OF RAIN AND EMERALD

THE WEATHER COURT GEM SERIES

KC SILVER

Copyright © 2025 by KC Silver.

All rights reserved.

No portion of this book may be reproduced in any form without written permission from the publisher or author, except as permitted by U.S. copyright law.

To those watching the rain pour: don't let fear stop you from getting
a little wet.

One

The sea breeze whipped Falov's hair, the long, brown locks attacking his face. He swiped the strands away from his mouth and sighed once he managed to pull them back with a leather tie.

Beyond the bow of the ship upon which he sailed, Nadmor—his hometown—splayed along the coastline. He was eager to sail away from the fishy stench of the stone streets, full of cracks that he tripped over countless times while too drunk to see clearly, stumbling back to his lodgings. The small room in the boarding house he occupied was lonely and dark, but it was enough to get him through the stints when he was back on land.

In the last year Falov had spent more time on sea than he had on land. He preferred the boarding house to living in that large manor with his mother who only battered him with complaints about his life's path, and reminded him of what they had lost. It wasn't their home anymore anyway—his mother was just a guest. Everything about that building tormented him, and he was glad that he had saved up enough coin over the years by helping his father to afford a place of his own.

Before he spiraled for too long, Falov turned to face his cage for the next month: *The Dark Destiny.*

Her black sails billowed in the wind, and he inhaled the salty sea air like it was his lifeline. Perhaps it was. He grew up sailing on this beauty his whole life, following his father around with his small sketchbook and drawing the scenes in front of him. Most of those sketches were now in the sea after he had tossed them overboard and let the waves swallow them whole.

A large hand clamped over Falov's shoulder. He wasn't startled by it, since he had heard the man's cane clink against the wood of the deck on his approach.

His uncle's familiar deep voice rumbled, "Skarb showed mercy on us today. Not a cloud in the sky."

Skarb—The God of the Rain Court. All sailors prayed to him before they set sail. Some for an easy passage, while others hoped for the thrilling adventure rough seas promised. But being in the Rain Court meant one thing was always certain.

"It won't last," Falov pointed out. "Skarb loves toying with us. I bet we'll have storms by nightfall."

Druz—his captain, his uncle, and his father's unplanned successor—outstretched a palm. "I'll throw my hand into that bet."

Falov looked around the ship, watching as the crew began to stow supplies and rig the sails. It would be a long month of sailing the seas and trying to find the emerald Heart of the court to win the Undertaking, a yearly trial to ensure the Rain court's survival. If none of the four competing ships found the Heart, the court would flood over and everyone would die. Including the mermaids, who would lose their tails, and thus not be able to survive the great drowning either.

Every year they faced the same threat of death as the court's minister hid the Heart in a secret location. This year there was a new minister who had taken on the mantle, and pirates were spreading rumors that it would be one of the toughest years to find the Heart. Pirates had been dictated as those who would sail to find the Heart because no other civilian would ever dare to pay the hefty entrance fee—one that left a deep scar.

Falov shook his head. "If we start making bets now, then the whole crew will want to join. Whoever loses is going to be in a pissy mood. We don't need that tension already."

His uncle chuckled, combing his fingers through his long gray beard as he, too, looked upon his ship. "Always thinking two steps ahead. That's why I made you my first mate."

"I'm your first mate because I'm the reason we're even able to compete this year."

"Well, killing a mermaid and stealing her heart makes you worthy of the role." Druz looked down at him, his eyes boring directly into his nephew's mind. Falov had to look away before his uncle started spouting about how proud he was.

The last year had been a blur, mainly because Falov had been drunk for most of it. It was the reason his uncle had even stepped up to be captain for *The Dark Destiny's* Undertaking voyage. It was meant for Falov now that his father had died, but his uncle, the crew, and his mother all agreed he wasn't in the right mindset. Falov had even overheard his mother saying she didn't think it was right for him to join the crew for the Undertaking, but Falov couldn't accept her coddling. Although he had previously joined *The Dark Destiny* on other voyages, this was his first time participating in the Undertaking because his mother had so adamantly refused to let him go, and his father had never denied her the request. She had excused it as a way to protect the future captain of *The Dark Destiny*; but if he had been on this ship a year ago, his father—along with other innocent crew members—would still be alive today.

Falov cleared his throat. "I should go make sure everything is set."

His uncle gripped the rail of the ship, keeping his frail body steady, and Falov choked down the guilt. Druz had to watch his younger brother die, and now he had to step up because Falov had been incapable of keeping it together over the last year. "It's about that time, isn't it?"

Falov hummed his acknowledgement, itching to leave Nadmor behind. He took one last glance at land, at those shops, and pubs, and the lives that depended on the pirates' bravery. His father had been enraptured by the calling to protect the court—with his brother and second family by his side—and Falov was patiently waiting for that same transcendent feeling.

"What did your mother say?" Druz asked.

Falov stopped in his tracks. "I didn't visit her."

Druz's disappointed face almost—*almost*—made Falov feel guilty, but he refused to allow that feeling to fester.

"She's vulnerable." His uncle's words punctured the hole in Falov's chest even more.

"She's grieving in her own way, like I am, too. I can't be the person she relies on when I can barely hold it together myself most days."

"At least you're honest." His uncle sighed. "But she has no one else."

Falov wasn't entertaining this conversation. Trying to untangle his relationship with his mother only resulted in a tighter knot. She refused to speak about her separation from his father and getting remarried to the former minister—the one who was now deceased. She refused to speak about her past at all, about her previous life as a mermaid—one of the many princesses, no less.

Falov noticed Lina, their helmsman, gesturing for Captain Druz. Although Lina's title put her under both Captain Druz and Falov, she had no problem commanding them both around to keep operations moving smoothly on the ship.

"It looks like Lina needs you," he grumbled to his uncle. Lina was another person he had a complicated—or more specifically, *contentious*—relationship with.

"Be prepared to leave soon. Perhaps at least write her a note," Druz warned before heading over to Lina, his pace slow as he leaned on his cane for balance across the deck. His uncle could walk without it, but he chose to use it on days when his pain was egregious.

Falov shrugged off his uncle's suggestion, and started towards the stern where his private quarters were. He didn't have spacious quarters like the Captain, but even a small room, only big enough to fit a cot, was better than sleeping with the rest of the crew in the communal bunks. Falov had experienced his fair share of nights trying to get comfortable in those hammocks and failing.

He nodded and smiled to a few of the crew members as he went, but he needed a moment of quiet before they set off on their journey. Once they were on the sea, with no land in sight, he would have no break from dealing with some problem or another. Captain Druz, Lina, Mora, and himself had discussed their first destination to search for the Heart, but each second on the sea would be unexpected. No amount of preparation could set them up for whatever the Gods had in store for them.

And no amount of daydreaming would ever prepare him for the sight of Syrena sitting on his bed, with only a thin, white sheet to cover her.

She tripped on the sheet, but she couldn't care less. She had the killer up against the wall with a rusty hook at his throat before he could even open his mouth.

"Where is it?" Syrena snarled.

His piercing blue eyes widened as he carefully stammered out, "What?"

"You know what you took." What he had stolen from her. What he had no right to take.

"I don't know what you're talking about," he said slowly against the sharp end, careful to avoid slicing his own throat.

"Don't play with me, Falov." She inched the tip closer, pressing it enough to break through his fragile, tanned skin. A small red bead pooled around the steel.

"Syrena," he gulped out. "Let's talk this out before you make any hasty moves you'll regret."

His hands snaked around until he could grab the wrist of the hand she held the hook with. He was trying to be reasonable, trying to get *her* to be reasonable. She wouldn't stand for that. Not after she trusted him enough to bring him to her home. Not after he killed her friend and stole her heart, just to be able to enter the Undertaking.

Falov would pay with his life.

She gripped the hook tighter and his eyes tracked the small movement. They trailed up her arm, to her hair, and directly to her brown eyes.

"I forgot how pretty you are."

She gritted her teeth. "Flattery won't stop me."

One of his hands let go of her to twirl the end of her long hair around his finger, the inky black and teal ends enveloping his tan skin. She caught a glimpse of the scars between his fingers, the ones she had cried for when she discovered why they were there.

"It might give you time to rethink." His voice was tight.

"I have been thinking of this moment for weeks," she spat. "Nothing will stop me."

His pupils were blown wide, and she could feel his rapid pulse beating. He was scared, and she thrived at the knowledge it was because of her. Yet it made her think of Nyphadora and her final moments. How scared and alone she must have been. Everyday, Syrena wished she could have stopped it. But at least she could get revenge in Nyphadora's honor.

"How about some water?"

Before she could react, the hands that were around her burst water all over them both, dousing the moonshell necklace hanging from her throat.

Syrena gasped as her legs began to tingle and shift, her scales clawing their to the surface of her skin. She stepped away, yanking the necklace off to the floor before her body betrayed her. Falov took advantage of her vulnerability and swiftly bound her wrists together with a rope. Though he didn't let go of her, as if he had recognized that ropes wouldn't be enough to hold her back for long.

"Now, now," he purred. "Why don't we be civil?"

She squirmed in his arms, her back to his chest, but the only thing she accomplished was rubbing her body against his.

"Let. Me. Go." She tried kicking him, but he caught her foot.

"Princess, you're caught in my net. You have no room for demands anymore."

His hot breath against her neck angered her even more. Months ago it would have driven her mad with desire. It was funny how quickly her feelings had changed.

"So be a good fisherman and let me go back swimming into the sea," she crooned, hoping for any leverage.

Even though she couldn't see him, she sensed his smile. "Perhaps I would enjoy eating you first."

"Not happening."

Voices sounded from the other side of the door, and Syrena froze. If she was caught by anyone else she would be dead immediately. Pirates hated mermaids and everything they represented, especially if they were on a ship destined for voyage for the Heart. It wasn't like mermaids were any less prejudiced. If a landwalker was caught in the sea, mermaids wouldn't hesitate to wrap their webbed hands around their throats and suck all the air from their lungs.

"I won't tell them who you are. What you are," Falov whispered.

"And what price must I pay for your discretion?"

"I need something from you." She could feel him shrug from behind her. "You have a skill that's useful for this particular task."

She knew what he spoke of immediately. All mermaids had the ability to lure with their songs, but only royalty had the innate ability to track.

She stilled in his arms. "You would open yourself up to being cursed by the Gods. To what? Prove yourself worthy?" She scoffed, disbelieving the way he was acting. This wasn't the Falov of the past, the one who couldn't care less about victory as long as everyone from *The Dark Destiny* was safe. "What will this crew think when they learn you're cheating?"

"They'd never find out."

"What if instead," she began, her voice turning sing-songy as an idea began to form, "you let me on this crew and keep my secret. At the end, you give me back what I want...and a slice of the treasure." She added the last part impulsively, but if she was going to be putting in the work, then she deserved something nice at the end of it.

It was Falov's turn to pause. "We would have to win." Syrena fidgeted in his arms, and he tightened his hold. "Which means you have to act sensibly. If we lose, Nyphadora's precious heart burns to ash."

"It's on this ship. What if I just steal it?"

He turned her around, their bodies so close together, that it would only take her leaning forward for their lips to brush. He seemed to sense her thoughts because his eyes trailed down to her mouth as she licked her lips.

His voice was low and dark, the vibrations hitting somewhere deep within her that she refused to give attention to. "Then *The Dark Destiny* will not only be tracking the emerald Heart but your head, too."

She growled, fisting her hands, refusing to accept this fate. She had left home expecting a quick mission, telling no one where she was headed.

"How can I trust you?"

And the way he flinched, Syrena knew she hit the mark she intended.

Wordlessly, he picked up her shell necklace and gently placed it over her head so it rested where it belonged. His hand lingered on the red shell, the same color as Nyphadora's scales. Every mermaid had the opportunity to travel the treacherous sea to find a moon-shell, imbued with the magic to shift to a landwalker. Syrena had gone with Nyphadora when they were both eight, surviving hungry sharks, angry old mermaids, and undersea currents ready to wipe them away just to find the shells they had dreamed of. Obtaining the shell came at a price; in order to stay a mermaid, Syrena needed to wear the necklace, and keep it hydrated. If the shell was parched for too long, she risked the possibility of never being able to shift back to what she had been born as.

"I'm not some scheming villain," Falov insisted so strongly that Syrena thought he not only was trying to assure her but himself, too.

"You murdered my friend."

His nostrils flared. *Good,* she thought. He deserved to be knocked down a few rungs.

"For this to work, you'll need to be willing to move aside that distrust."

"Fine." She gritted her teeth, but it wasn't so simple. Although Falov appeared exactly the same from the last time she saw him, when they had so blissfully held each other in his room at that boarding house, she didn't see him the same way anymore. Not after she had received news of Nyphadora's murder and the minister's death.

Falov gave her a flat smile, as if he too felt wrong about his demands.

He crossed his arms. "Like I said, you would be expected to participate like any other crew member on this ship. To clean, to cook, to help with whatever task Captain Druz says."

She rolled her eyes. "I'll sneak out at night and catch a few fish for you all." Even though she didn't eat it herself, she needed to shift back to her mermaid form regularly enough anyway.

"So you agree? You'll help us track the Heart, and I promise to somehow ensure you get Nyphadora's heart back."

"Well now you don't seem so confident you'll get me what I want," she mumbled.

"Semantics," he brushed it off. "I have connections."

Once again, she tried pulling her hands out of the shackled ropes around her wrist and failed, the knots too tight. Her shoulders sagged. Her family would be concerned about her disappearance, but they weren't her priority right now. She didn't have a fully formed idea mapped out, but she did know one thing: if she stuck close to Falov, she would have the power to ensure this crew never won the Heart, and that would be the ultimate retribution.

This ship wasn't endless. Nyphadora's heart was somewhere, and Syrena would get it if she had to tear the ship apart board by board.

She lifted her chin. He looked unsure of this, and that pleased her.

She smiled. "I guess it's time to introduce the newest member of *The Dark Destiny.*"

Two

Regret pooled in Falov's chest. He didn't know what came over him, but the mixture of her sweet scent and her warm body against his brought him back to when they'd been tangled together in his sheets, the world outside nothing but a blur. Everyday since then he had craved her touch. Some—namely his uncle and the crew—would have called him a fool for messing around with a mermaid. They would blame his unquenchable desire on her siren song, but it wasn't that. Syrena had an aura around her, and he couldn't escape its clutch. Her long, dark hair that gradated to a teal. Her supple skin. Her iridescent, white tail that was easy to spot even in the darkest depths of the sea. Every facet of her was like a shiny jewel, worth more to him than the emerald Heart of the Rain Court.

Unfortunately, she clearly wanted him dead.

Could he blame her? Not really. He *had* killed Nyphadora, and no amount of guilt or justification would ever change that. He remembered the aftermath of that moment, the way his body shook. His mother had held him tight, her hot tears dripping onto his clothes. His voice had wavered as he'd sobbed Syrena's name, and his mother nodded in understanding. Together they wrote the news of Nyphadora's death, stuffed it in a bottle, and gave it to a mermaid courier to be sent off to her loved ones. He hadn't heard from or seen Syrena since.

"Let's get you in some real clothes." The white sheet wrapped around her as an impromptu dress would raise too many brows.

She looked down at herself as if she'd forgotten. Then she turned around, revealing her still-tied hands. "I won't be able to do much like this."

"Do you promise not to do anything rash while I steal some clothes from Lina?"

"No," Syrena responded without hesitation. He sighed and muttered profanities to himself. Skarb spare him. This voyage was doomed already.

Falov untied the knots, a sign he was willing to trust her. As soon as he did, she pulled the sheet off her body, leaving her completely bare in front of him. He swallowed, keeping his focus on her eyes, even if this might be the last time he would ever see her unclothed. He sometimes forgot how brazen the seafolk were.

"I'll be right back," he said under his breath, quickly turning away. He shut the door quietly, hoping no one would investigate his quarters.

Since Lina was still on deck, it was easy to nab a pair of brown pants and a loose white shirt from her things. They weren't really hers, just leftovers from her couplings. Lina liked treasure, but she also liked luring lovers into her bed.

When he returned, Syrena had not covered herself, but she had clearly been snooping. She had one of his sketchbooks in her hand, and was flipping through the art. His first instinct was to snatch it away but that would only feed her curiosity. So he kept still and let her finish. While he waited, his eyes roved over her exposed flesh. Even though she looked completely human, the way her body curved, moving like the lithe waves of the sea, revealed the true mermaid beneath.

Syrena slammed the sketchbook shut and reached out to grab the clothes. Their fingers brushed as they exchanged items, and he could feel her breath stall. His own became labored, a flood of desire coursing through him. It had always been that way between them, an instantaneous heat neither of them could explain—*wanted* to explain. They had always reveled in the strong tide that was *them*, appreciating it in awe. Their eyes connected, but he pulled away before his body acted on that instinct.

"I'll wait outside the door. When you're dressed, we can go tell the crew."

She didn't say anything, so he left her to it, before he started having the urge to explain himself like he'd had for months. Knowing her—and he did know her—she wouldn't want to listen, because when she had a grudge against someone, she held it tight. He would be wasting his breath.

Plus, he needed to figure out an excuse for her presence. Syrena wouldn't require too many supplies since she could always go down to the sea, and like she had suggested, she would be valuable because she would be able to catch them fresh food. But the crew would only see her as another mouth to feed and another life at stake.

He never planned to tell the crew about her true form because it was decreed that using a mermaid—especially royals with tracking abilities—was cheating, and that made the crew susceptible to being cursed by the Weather Gods. The seafolk's special abilities were the reason they could not participate in the Undertaking. It would be considered too easy, according to the Gods. And the Gods were cruel. They wanted a show each year, where the court was on a rocky edge, fearing for their lives. Falov thought it unfair that in order to enter into the Undertaking, a pirate needed to kill one of the seafolk, while mermaids could not participate themselves if they wanted to. Others excused it easily, deeming mermaids replaceable since they reproduced at a faster pace than landwalkers, while some justified it by how mermaids had no qualms murdering landwalkers either.

The door opened and there she was.

The pants were too big and she used a rope as a belt. The shirt was tied on the side and tucked in. But even in something so plain, she looked ethereal.

When he reached her eyes, they were on him. He cleared his throat before he started drooling.

"Let's go." He lowered his voice to sound more commanding but it only resulted in a huff of annoyance from her.

She shoved past him, leading the way instead of following him. *That* he wouldn't let slip by. He grabbed her hand and tugged her back until she stumbled into his arms. He had her pressed against the wall in an instant.

"You are the bottom of the barrel on this ship. You will be expected to listen to Captain Druz, and since I am his first mate, you will listen to me, too."

"What happened to you?" The words were sharp and quick.

The question rocked him, but he remained focused on her.

"You never cared about title and power," she continued. "The Falov I knew would never kill, and he never wanted to lead. Your heart is rotting."

He blinked, letting the insult pass. "It's not that simple." And he didn't owe her an explanation when she would be resistant to the truth. As much as he desperately wanted to tell her what transpired that day, he owed it to them both to do it when they were each ready. He just hoped that opportunity would one day exist.

Her assessing glare had him pulling away again. He didn't like when she tried to read him. He hated it even more when she was the only one who knew that becoming captain was not his dream, but a future that had been thrust upon him.

"We're weighing the anchor soon. We should introduce you before we do."

Her smirk was cold and shallow. She took her necklace from around her neck and hid it in her pocket. "Lead the way, First Mate Falov."

One thing Syrena hated more than the man in front of her was being ordered around—but for Nyphadora, she would endure whatever the next month would bring. Though she hoped she could accomplish her goal in less time than that. How hard could it be to trick a group of pirates?

They made it to the deck of the ship and immediately the salty sea air revived her senses. She could feel the water around her and how it called to her. She wondered if Falov had the same feeling. From what she knew, his kernel of seafolk power was small, inconsequential in comparison to full-blooded mermaids. Yet, he was able to manifest a burst large enough to impact her shifting. Had he lied to her all those months ago when she climbed into his bed? His mother was a former princess, so it made sense her offspring would have strong gifts of the sea, despite having given up her tail.

"If we don't leave soon, we'll be behind." A boy who appeared no older than eight bounced on his feet as he complained to a small group of people standing around the rear of the ship. Other crew members busily passed by, stowing crates into the hull or adjusting the rigging.

One of them—a woman whose gray eyes showed signs of experience—yanked the boy's shaggy, blond hair.

"You ought to learn patience if you ever want to be a member of the crew, Luga."

"I *am* a member of the crew" He rubbed his head. His clothes were too small on his growing frame but it didn't seem to bother him.

"Being a cabin boy hardly makes you an official member," someone else teased with a smile, and Luga pouted at the insult.

"Shouldn't you be mopping the decks as we speak?"

Luga opened his mouth to retort, but Falov stepped in. "Let's not harass the kid already. Especially you, Lina. I expect better from you."

Lina crossed her arms, her short leather vest showing off her toned arms. As Syrena neared, she noticed the necklace Lina wore. The shiny red scales glimmered in the sunlight. The same as Nyphadora's fiery scales—the ones Syrena could recognize from anywhere. Where did this bitch get them?

Something in Syrena's demeanor must have changed because Falov's hand pressed against the small of her back. Syrena looked down at herself and realized her hands were clenched so tight her nails were biting into her skin. She relaxed them.

While Syrena assessed Lina, the rest of the group had their eyes on her. She forced her face neutral, refusing to give any one of them room to make any assumptions about her. Showing that hint of anger already left her too exposed.

"Who's the imposter?" another crew member asked. This one looked like she was pulled directly out of the sun. Her bright yellow hair and eyes glowed so intensely it made Syrena's own pupils sizzle.

"This is Syrena," Falov awkwardly introduced, "an old friend—and your new right hand, Mora." Falov turned to Syrena. "Mora is our navigator, but since you have a knack for finding things, you can provide additional guidance when you're not busy helping with other tasks."

Syrena stayed silent. She wouldn't give him the satisfaction of showing her agreement.

"She looks like one of the seafolk," Lina accused as she spat on the wooden deck.

Syrena had to keep from cringing.

"You think everyone is seafolk, and you're always wrong," Falov reasoned.

"Let's throw her overboard and test it out then." Lina smiled coldly, her gray eyes swirling like storm clouds.

Syrena didn't know what was wrong with this woman, but Syrena could tell Lina would make her life difficult—so she didn't feel bad when she said, "Why don't we start with you first?"

"Excuse me?"

Everyone around them seemed to freeze as if any disruption would only cause Lina to explode. Even Falov didn't stop it.

"Nice necklace," Syrena spat as she approached Lina, gathered the necklace in her hand and inspected it closely. "Especially those scales. Only seafolk would be able to gift you those...or you're a mermaid in disguise."

"How dare you question me?" Lina seethed. But Syrena shrugged flippantly because not giving Lina the reaction she craved left the most delicious taste in her mouth.

"What in the Gods is going on here?" a deep voice snarled from behind her.

The rest of the group all turned their attention to the new voice, but Syrena didn't. She guessed immediately that it must be Captain Druz. Only someone in charge would be able to hold a room—or in this case, the deck of a ship—with such fervor.

His footsteps stomped until he circled to face Syrena. He was holding a cane, but he hadn't been using it, as if he wanted to prove he didn't need it. The man wasn't entirely what she expected. Tall, long beard, commanding though old. She could see the years of fatigue, the strenuous labor he'd put himself through. The limp showed he had fought and survived, but he was no longer fit to be captain on such a dangerous journey.

"Who is this?" Captain Druz directed the question at Falov by pointing at him with his cane.

Oh, these people would learn to respect her.

"Syrena," she answered before Falov could.

No one moved but there was a communal cringe amongst the crew. Syrena didn't care.

The Captain finally looked at her. "Why are you here?"

"Falov called in a favor. I'm here to deliver."

Falov was now at her side. "She's here because I asked."

"I was not consulted," The Captain said.

"I was on my way to speak to you when things…turned tense." He side-eyed Lina, but she only smiled widely.

The Captain gestured in front of him, indicating Falov had the floor to speak. "Why exactly do we need someone who clearly has never been on a ship?"

Syrena prepared to defend herself, but Falov clasped her forearm. His touch was warm and familiar. She wanted to shove him away, but her body wouldn't let her. Everyone clocked his movement, but he only spoke directly to his captain.

"She has an innate knack for tracking. She'd be a valuable asset to finding the Heart."

"Sounds like seafolk," Lina coughed under her breath.

"Why would I bring seafolk onto this ship when I'm the one who killed a mermaid so we can compete?"

Those words, the reminder of what he had done, made Syrena shift away. Only slightly, but she knew Falov noticed it. They were not allies. Neither of them were foolish enough to think that. She had a goal she planned to accomplish and a heart she wanted back. Whoever got tossed overboard as she attained her goals was not her problem.

Falov continued, "I would never risk this crew getting cursed."

No one seemed to rally behind him, but Captain Druz seemed too tired to push back.

"She stays in your room. And if she causes any trouble, you're responsible." Captain Druz then addressed everyone else, his voice booming. "We set sail in five."

The Captain limped away, calling Lina with him. The woman gave Syrena one last cold look before following Captain Druz. The others took that as a cue to disperse, leaving Syrena and Falov awkwardly alone together

"Please don't make my life difficult." His voice sounded tired.

Syrena didn't understand. Why was he so desperate to win the Heart? So much so that he was risking it all by allowing her to join. She flipped through her memories but could think of nothing that would have spurred him to act so irrationally.

"I'm your docile servant." She bowed mockingly. "Perhaps after this you can take my heart as your new trophy, too. Start a collection, even."

"I'm not your enemy."

"And you aren't my savior either. You're nobody to me."

Falov flinched, but she didn't care. Once, she imagined they meant something to each other, but he had betrayed her trust. Nothing would win it back.

She left him on the deck, leaving to find Luga to see if he needed any help. Being around Falov took a toll on her very soul. She could simply end the torment and enact her revenge now—but she wanted to play the long game, to get his walls down. Only then, when he was vulnerable, would she rip his heart from his chest and take back everything he'd stolen.

Three

Syrena spent the whole day with Luga either scrubbing the deck on her hands and knees or lugging crates of food into a storage room that definitely had something rotting in the dusty back corner. Luga had been chatty, revealing small secrets, like how one of the crew members slept with a blanket from childhood, or how another had two lovers waiting for him back on land. Apparently, Lina had revealed this to the two women right before they set sail so that when they returned, he would be welcomed with an unpleasant surprise.

Out of all her tasks, the most embarrassing was serving the crew their bowls of stew. None of the crew seemed to trust her. All of them took small bites, like they were suspicious that she had poisoned the meal. A part of her wished she had.

Falov kept away from her the whole day, as if a contagious plague festered under her skin. He joked with the crew, gave orders that they respected, and even let Luga steer the ship for an hour while he supervised. It was all laughable, honestly. He was the proven murderer here, yet not a single person cared. Landwalkers never did. The seafolk were just collateral for their stupid need to win the

Undertaking—and by extension, the treasure. Trinkets, gold, jewels. That was enough of a prize for them to excuse a taken life.

While the rest of them scarfed down their food, Syrena headed down to the hull of the ship to go...she supposed she didn't know where. If she was smart with her time, she would have searched the ship for Nyphadora's heart. But her body had been drained from all the labor. She wasn't used to working like this in her human form.

She tapped her foot, looking around aimlessly. She had no desire to sleep alongside the rest of the crew. They had a target on her back. Plus she would need to get on and off the boat during the night in order to ensure she could let her tail soak so she didn't get stuck as a human. Mermaids could last on land for two days before the powers of the shell they wore dried up and their change to a landwalker became permanent. But the symptoms began sooner, warning her of the impending shift—her skin would begin to peel, and her mouth would become parched. She preferred to avoid those sensations.

She heard footsteps clambering down the stairs. They were uneven and loud, and she knew it was Falov. He told her once he injured his leg during a brutal storm, and ever since, he slightly limped on his left leg if he worked too much on it.

"You're sleeping with me," he explained. His tone was even, but it wasn't the same voice he used with the others. With the crew, there was an edge of authority. But with her, there was an underlying care. It made her insides squirm.

"I'd rather sleep with the fish," Syrena muttered.

He was right behind her now. "That isn't saying much when you're basically a fish yourself."

She whipped around to face him, poking a long finger at his chest. "Don't insult me or my kind."

He put his hands up in surrender, his scars on full display. "We should go into my quarters before anyone overhears."

"I don't want to be anywhere near you," she snapped. She wasn't proud of how she let her emotions surface, but his presence invoked her baser instincts.

"If you want Nyphadora's heart, then you'll follow me."

Her mouth gaped open, but he only side-stepped her and started for his quarters. She could do nothing but obey.

"You're cruel."

"I have a ship of people I'm responsible for."

She huffed a dry laugh. "You're not captain yet."

"My uncle isn't in the right shape for this voyage. I'm captain in all ways except the title."

"You wouldn't be responsible for anybody if you weren't participating in this foolish Undertaking."

He turned around, squinting at her. "Someone has to do it, Syrena. It isn't just our lives at stake, but yours too. This whole court depends on pirates to save us for another year."

"Is that what you say to make yourself feel better?"

"I'm truly sorry Nyphadora had to die—"

"Don't you dare say her name," Syrena seethed. "And don't you even think your half-hearted apology will *ever* make up for killing my only friend. I'm here for her heart and that is all."

His shoulders deflated, the edge of frustration that had begun to seep out had been sucked back in. "Then let's meet in my room to strategize our first move."

Once again, they were at a standstill. She knew being stubborn would only prolong her from achieving her goal, but she couldn't move past her hatred.

Just then the ship swayed forcefully and Syrena lost her footing. She plunged forward, bracing for a fall, but Falov caught her by the waist. Before she could shove him away, he lifted her up over his shoulder.

"Put me down!" She smacked his strong back, formed from years of working on the ship. She shook her hand, wincing at the pain that shot up her arm.

"I will when we're in my room."

"You're despicable."

"And you're being difficult."

"I think I'm allowed to cause you some frustration."

He heaved as he tossed her down on the cot. In her attempt to escape his hold, she had untucked his loose shirt from his pants, exposing his chest to her. She forced herself not to look at the lean muscles beneath.

"Maybe you're right. But not when it comes at the expense of this crew. I will not have anything stand in the way of getting this Heart."

"What happened?" she asked genuinely, trying to understand. "A year ago, you were saying the Undertaking is a cruel test from the Gods. That your father was journeying on a foolish endeavor. That you wished you wouldn't need to take up the mantle of captain."

"It *is* foolish, and I *am* being a fool."

"So why?"

"For his honor," he replied before he quickly changed the subject. "Mora suggested the Rafa Reefs as a first stop."

Syrena stared at him. His father had died. No wonder he was so bent on winning. From the numerous conversations they had in the past, Falov had always detested the Undertaking and what it cost his father to participate each year. He resented it even more because he couldn't be there with the crew as they faced the treacherous sea so he could help them. All he wanted was for his father to finally win so that he could move on from that gnawing obsession. Yet...that contempt wasn't enough to stop Falov from taking his father's mantle, and killing a mermaid.

"Then we go with her suggestion."

He narrowed his eyes. "Are your powers directing you that way?"

"No, but I think supporting Mora's direction this first round will get her to at least warm up to me. None of them," she pointed upwards, "will just listen to me on a whim."

"So there is a reasonable bone in your body then."

She wouldn't take the bait. She was growing tired, and she still needed to go down to the sea and get some food.

"Go rest, Falov."

"But—"

"You know I can't be on land for too long."

"I'll take you to the gundeck. You can jump out of the gun port so no one sees you."

Her pride would hate it, but she relented. He would make sure no one tried anything and that she wasn't sighted shifting into the water. She tapped her pocket, ensuring her shell necklace was still inside.

They passed by a few crewmembers and each gave her a skeptical look, but she refused to show any sign of discomfort. Luckily, the gundeck was empty, though the smoky and pungent smell of sulfur made her gag.

"You aren't going to ditch me, are you?" Falov asked.

"Do I have Nyphadora's heart?"

"No."

"So you still have what I need. That should be enough insurance that I'll be back."

"And hopefully when I see you next that frown will have turned into a jovial smile."

"Or I can kill you in your sleep," Syrena deadpanned.

"I guess I deserve that," he sighed. "Happy swimming, Syrena."

She didn't like how regretful and resigned those words sounded. As she watched him go, there was a stabbing sensation in her chest. She rubbed at it, but ignored the feeling in favor of hanging the necklace around her neck. She took off her clothes, and dove into the water, where the sea welcomed her with its open arms.

Back on deck, Falov monitored the crew. On the crow's nest, a crew member stood to take the first watch, his spyglass aimed at the horizon instead of the sea, where Syrena had jumped. Others stood in groups, drinking rum from flasks to celebrate the start of their voyage. Two pirates on the poop deck slashed wooden swords at each other. They were drunk, no doubt, but since there was no actual blade attached to those hilts, Falov let their idiocy slide. It would be the only night for a while that Falov would allow them to indulge. His uncle was less strict, but he allowed Falov to make the call since he was the reason they could participate in this year's Undertaking. Hence, he would ensure his crew was always clear-minded because he would not have a repeat of last year. His father had allowed his obsession with winning to take over, and he made stupid and dangerous decisions as a result.

He joined the group with Mora and Lina. He could tell from their red-tinted cheeks that they had been drinking for a while.

"Falov!" Lina shouted. "Take a swig."

She offered him the bottle, but he turned it down. He knew Captain Druz was in his quarters already, so there was someone else not partaking in the festivities, but Falov preferred to stay alert. The sea wasn't predictable enough for him to let his guard down. Falov was shocked that Lina was participating—she usually kept alert, too.

He shook his head, and even in a hazy state, Lina knew to respect his wishes. She shrugged, passing off the drink to the next person in line.

"What's got you so broody?" Mora crooned, though her words slurred. "Is it that girl?"

Mora looked behind Falov, as if she expected Syrena to pop out from behind a barrel.

"She's resting," he responded.

"I don't trust her," Mora pouted.

"You barely trust yourself," Lina said, as she ran a finger over her scale necklace. For the first time Falov wondered how Lina had it in her possession. He wanted to ask, but he figured it would be best to wait when they were in private. Trying to get Lina to talk to him was like walking the plank: although it felt secure, any second she might shake the board beneath his feet until he fell. "Though, I don't trust her either. That hair looks fishy—and I mean that literally."

Mora clucked her tongue before taking a swig of the rum as it was handed to her. Wiping her mouth, she said accusatorily, "You had red hair once upon a time."

Lina's fingers combed through her black hair, and smoothed over the shaved underside. She sighed, gazing out at the dark sea. "That was when I was directionless and young."

"Until I entered your life and led you on the correct path?"

"Your cunt is not that magical," Lina sniped. "*The Dark Destiny* was my real guiding light."

"Syrena agrees with your direction, Mora." Falov chimed in, not wanting to hear their drunk blabberings. Mora and Lina's history was vague to him. He was a child when they joined his father's crew, but he did know they had some sort of fling that later grew into a strong friendship with no weird tension between them thankfully. Frankly, he didn't know too much about the crew's lives once they stepped off *The Dark Destiny*.

"See?" Mora pointed to Lina. "The girl has a mind after all."

Lina rolled her eyes. "Let's hope you're right. Sailing to the reefs is a dangerous game."

The Rafa Reefs were venerated by the seafolk as a wonder from the Weather Gods. Any pirate, person, or animal that seeked to destroy it would be eaten and killed on the spot. They would have to be careful and take the rowboats out once they neared it.

"So it's settled," Falov brought his hands together, grateful at least that they had a direction for their first stop.

He didn't know what the next month would bring. It would be full of rocky seas, mood swings, and disappointment, no doubt. Yet, deep in his gut, as the salty wind blew through his hair, he sensed the Undertaking would change him. Last year's Undertaking brought death and grief. This year he aimed for pride and accomplishment so that he could avenge his father and make his crew proud.

Four

Even though it had only been a mere few hours since she had swam the seas, it was still a breath of relief when she was reunited with her iridescent, white tail and webbed hands. The deep blue surrounded her, but even at night, she could still see her world crisp and clear. When she was younger, she imagined that the sea was the sky and that she was flying through the air. Nyphadora and her would pretend the fish were birds, and they would chase them around.

Once she acquired her shell necklace and explored the land above, she pitied the landwalkers because they would never experience the true wonders of the sea. There were markets where sellers procured troves of goods from shipwrecks or visits above, performances done by the most talented singers—because although all mermaids had the luring song, only some actually sounded good to other mermaids' ears. There was a whole society that landwalkers were excluded from because they didn't have the power.

Well...except for a rare few. One of them being Falov.

During their temporary romantic fling—because that's all it was to her now, all it *could* be now—Syrena invited him to join her under the sea. He could only last about an hour with his bubble of air, but it was enough time for him to become acquainted with a world that was innately a part of him. Those scars between his fingers proved how the seafolk side of him wanted to claw its way out—despite the fact that his parents had taken him to a physician to get the webbing removed. Yet even after experiencing the depths of the sea with her, Falov had committed to life as a landwalker.

As much as she wanted to swim home and to explain her absence, she couldn't. Her parents would reprimand her for interfering with the Undertaking and for risking herself. Also...the thought of being home in that large castle without her friend left a hollow ache. Sometimes Syrena thought the sea no longer felt like home without Nyphadora. Nothing was the same without her. Syrena missed her boisterous laugh and unwavering kindness. Even in those last few weeks where Nyphadora seemed distracted, she always found time to meet Syrena in their secret place to gossip and catch up. Syrena told her about Falov, nervous that Nyphadora would look down on her, but her friend cheered them on.

The most painful thing was she didn't have Nypahdora's heart to give her the proper sendoff because that bastard and his crew on *The Dark Destiny* thought they had a right to it. Her anger swelled, and she was reminded of why exactly she even agreed to be a crew member on that blasted ship: to interfere with their chances of winning.

Her hands fisted at her sides, and she was unable to breathe easily. How could she have trusted Falov?

It had been so easy to get pulled into his world on land. It was so different. The paved roads were small and crowded. The smells were pungent. The people were busy and tired, yet determined.

It wasn't special or wonderful. It was mundane. Yet Syrena couldn't get enough of it. She would be there everyday with Nyphadora at her side, trying new delicacies from the market. They had saved up enough coin over the years from scouring shipwrecks to splurge. But one day Nyphadora hadn't joined her, claiming she was too tired. Syrena went without her, and sat by the ports with a flaky roll. A young man was sitting not too far away with a large sketchpad and some charcoal in hand, entirely transfixed by whatever he was doing.

Curious, Syrena walked over, her steps light. She stood behind him and was surprised to see herself mirrored on the page. When he shifted his head, he didn't seem startled by her presence, but she was immediately enamored by those damn blue eyes.

"Isn't it a bit rude to draw someone without their permission?" she had quipped.

Falov had shrugged. "I'd rather be called rude than miss the chance to draw the most beautiful woman in existence."

Syrena had blushed, flustered by the compliment—which only made him chuckle, his head falling back, those long brown waves shining in the rare sunlight. She had crossed her arms, not as amused, but he patted the spot next to him.

"To make it even, I'll let you draw me."

That had sparked her interest enough, but they both quickly learned that she was awful at drawing. They had laughed until tears escaped their eyes.

Syrena blinked, bringing her back to the present. It was too much to think about right now. Pulling a stalk of seaweed, she stuffed it in her mouth and swallowed it down, the salty taste lingering on her tongue. She munched on more until she was satisfied. It wasn't the luxurious food she had at the castle, but it was enough to fill her up.

Overhead a dark shadow eclipsed the moonlight that penetrated through the water. She craned her neck up as an idea washed through her.

She propelled herself up, towards the large ship. Climbing the ladder, her body immediately responded by shifting to her human form when the shell necklace was no longer submerged. She was naked again, but she didn't plan on staying long. When she had climbed high enough to see the deck, there were a few pirates standing guard. Some appeared drunk, especially with the way they stumbled. In the corner, one of them played a flute. Syrena smiled.

Then, she sang, matching the notes of the instrument but allowing her voice to overtake the instrument's volume.

As the first note escaped her lips, those close enough to hear her straightened immediately, falling into a dreamlike trance. Her words conveyed her message, where they should go, who they would find.

Once her tune ended, the pirates all slumped back into their normal states. She didn't stay to watch them jump into action. She dove into the water, her flesh returning to a flurry of scales.

If all went to plan, she would be swimming back home with Nyphadora's heart soon. Then, she could finally move on from this horror and never think about Falov again.

Falov shot up from his cot, sensing something amiss. Syrena was nowhere to be found, but he didn't expect otherwise. He almost tripped over himself as he tried tugging on his pants in the tight space, but managed to get out of his quarters unscathed.

Aside from the waves crashing against the hull, the ship was quiet. He knew there was a group of the crew standing watch and that they would blast the horn if something was wrong, but he couldn't relinquish the nagging sensation pulsing through his chest. It urged him towards the deck.

He wouldn't sound the alarm until he had his sights on the sea.

One of the crew members who was flipping a coin as he leaned against the mast gave him a curious look. Falov hurried over to him.

"Have there been any signs of trouble?"

"No, sir. The water has been smooth so far."

"And you haven't seen Syrena?"

"The girl from earlier?" he stammered.

"Yes, the woman from earlier."

"No, it's just been me, Wysp, and Luga tonight."

Falov turned his attention up towards the crow's nest where Wysp was looking through a spyglass.

Everything seemed fine, yet Falov couldn't let go of urgency that had rocked him awake.

"Keep a close eye on everything."

The crew member nodded frantically, taking out his own spyglass to keep a closer eye.

Falov headed back down, but as he took one last peek out towards the water, he saw something move in the distance.

"Wysp!" he yelled out. Wysp's head popped out of the crow's nest. Falov pointed. "What is that?"

The man didn't hesitate to check, but Falov didn't need verbal confirmation to know there was a ship heading towards them by how Wysp froze.

"Sound the horn!" Falov warned.

Luga, who had been reading a book, tossed it aside and ran up to Falov.

"What can I do?" his small voice asked.

"Find somewhere safe and stay out of the way." Falov wouldn't be responsible for the kid getting killed.

"But—"

"Don't cross me, Luga. Captain Druz would give the same orders." Before Luga could complain again, Falov went to alert his uncle and the rest of the crew.

Lina was already awake and climbing up to the deck with Mora right behind her. Both of them had sobered up.

"Captain Druz!" Falov knocked on his door. "Trouble is heading our way."

Falov heard the crashing of something falling over. Falov considered opening the door and helping his uncle, but right when his hand grasped the doorknob, it was yanked away. Captain Druz leaned against the doorjamb, his coat and hat in hand, his cane missing. "Let's remind some pirates how *The Dark Destiny* got its name."

Peace turned to chaos in a matter of minutes. Falov ran to the gundeck where there were already crew members loading cannonballs into cannons. Others ran for the guns in the armory.

Falov first noted Syrena's clothes on the ground, and hid them deeper in a corner so no one noticed. It was both a relief and a curse that she hadn't returned yet.

He shook his head, scolding himself. He couldn't think about her now. At least underwater she was safe. That was his only comfort and it had to do.

Securing possession of a gun, he returned to the deck where the situation was more dire than he had expected. The other ship was closing in behind them, and they were ready to attack. Falov hated being on defense.

Swearing under his breath, he approached the wheel where Captain Druz was rotating the ship so the cannons would face the opposing ship.

"We should strike first," Falov recommended to his captain.

His uncle shook his head. "We wait."

A gust of wind attacked, destabilizing Falov, but he secured his feet on the deck.

"If they get a good hit at us before we can hit them, then we're screwed."

"We wait," the Captain repeated, his voice stern and final.

His uncle had been navigating the sea longer than Falov had been alive. He taught his brother—Falov's dad—everything he knew. Falov trusted Druz more than anything, but that didn't mean he had to agree with his approach.

Falov couldn't bite his tongue. They had to act. "You told me you wanted to give me more responsibility, so let me make this call."

That got the man's attention. He brushed his fingers through his gray beard. "The crew's safety should be your guiding light. At every turn, think of them."

It was a lesson many of them learned the hard way last year. Falov nodded and ran off before his uncle could revoke his permission. Lina was relaying orders below, positioning everyone properly. Falov bounded up to her, calling as he neared, "Tell them to aim and get ready to fire."

"But Captain Druz said—"

"I'm giving orders."

She opened her mouth, but shut it when she glanced up at Captain Druz. She didn't seem pleased by listening to Falov, but her choices were minimal.

"Where are we aiming?"

"Rigging. Only one cannon for now. We're fighting to disarm and warn, not to kill."

Lina nodded and immediately started passing off the order. Falov, being an idiot, cast a glance over the deck. There was no iridescent glow to be found. He didn't know why he expected her to show up and help. She hated him for a good reason. She must know they were being attacked and savoring it.

Focusing again, the crew was ready. Falov counted down and the cannon exploded. They all watched the cannonball fly with anticipation. It struck the other ship mid-mast. They didn't have a second to indulge in victory because a rival cannon blast was coming their way.

"Go!" Falov shouted at his uncle, who knew this tactic well. The ship was sailing fast, the wind in its sail pushing it quickly—though not fast enough to avoid a direct hit.

Falov's eyes widened once he noticed who was in the cannon's path.

"Luga!" Falov hissed as he slid on his knees to reach the young boy and cover them both from the flying fragments of wood.

The Dark Destiny swayed with the impact. As soon as it settled, Falov scrambled off of the boy, assessing the damage, breathing in relief when only the deck's railing had been splintered.

Falov hauled Luga to his feet, clasped his shoulders, and reprimanded him. "Get the fuck off the deck, kid. Go to the captain's quarters and stay there." There were tears in the boy's eyes, but Falov had no time to comfort him. Luga ran off, and Falov called for the next cannon. It didn't hit the opposing ship cleanly like their first shot had, but it still afforded *The Dark Destiny* a few precious seconds.

Back at the gundeck, Falov watched the crew prepare the cannons again. This time, they loaded the rear gun ports. His goal was to avoid shooting any more cannons, but they needed to be prepared. His father would have never let the back of the ship be exposed like this. He would have stationed the ship and fought until one of the ships was down. But that was how his body was rotting at the bottom of the sea—his father never knew when to give up.

He was moving around the ship like a fish stuck inside a glass encasement, running up and down the deck to get orders across. He heaved a deep breath as Mora came up to him, her own breaths shallow and reeking of alcohol.

"Falov, were only twenty kilometers away from the reefs. If we keep heading this way, our attackers will be the least of our worries."

"I know." He understood exactly where they were headed and how to stop the opposing ship from attacking them more.

Lina, overhearing their conversation, crossed her arms, almost like she wanted to see him fail. "So what's the plan?"

"No matter how crazy it gets, don't stop shooting," he commanded, then turned around to his uncle who was at the wheel. It was as if it had some magical properties because from here, he looked like a young and spry pirate. "Captain Druz! We're going to be making a sharp turn."

His uncle nodded, not even questioning Falov's strategy.

"When I say go," Falov spoke to the crew as loudly as he could. "We attack."

The ship became still, like the world around them took a deep breath in. The oncoming ship was moving quickly, while Captain Druz had slowed down to be able to execute the turn without capsizing his ship. Falov peered through the spyglass and saw the opposing ship preparing to strike again. They were close enough now that if they got a good hit in, *The Dark Destiny* would be irreparably damaged.

"Falov," Mora warned, as she stood at the ready with a gun. "They're getting too fucking close."

"Not yet."

The ship came closer and closer, and they seemed to be holding off, too, as if they were curious how *The Dark Destiny* would play this out.

They were right on their tail, and it would soon be a massacre if they didn't act. Yet Falov waited one second more.

Then he exhaled. "Go!"

Five

Syrena flipped through the water, following *The Dark Destiny* as it raced away from the onslaught. She had no idea what they were doing and why they were heading directly towards the Rafa Reefs. If they kept going at their current speed, they would strike the sacred ecosystem. Rival pirates would become least of their concerns if mermaids charged the ship.

As Syrena swam closer—and considered climbing aboard to demand Falov halt the ship—it made a sudden turn.

She stopped in her tracks, but the other ship trailing behind *The Dark Destiny* continued to charge ahead. It was going to destroy the reefs.

Fuck. She hadn't anticipated her plan going in this direction. As much as she didn't care about the lives of any pirate on these ships, as much as she would savor seeing the seafolk enact punishment on those who dared destroy the reefs, she didn't want to be the root of its destruction. If news ever spread that one of the princesses of the sea had been involved—much less the sole cause—she would be stripped of her tail.

Angry at whoever's idea it was to lure the opposing ship this way, Syrena took action. *The Dark Destiny* was already on a separate path, going parallel to the shallow water that housed the reefs. She needed to find a way to get the other ship to turn around, away from the reefs. Her song could not maneuver them fast enough. She needed to manipulate the water somehow. Although she had magic to do that, it would be easier if she had more hands.

She closed her eyes as she realized there was another person nearby with those exact gifts.

She swam fast, not allowing herself to hesitate. The longer she stalled, the less chance there was of this plan working.

Hoisting herself up the ladder, she crawled quietly aboard, knowing the gundeck must be rampant with activity. She needed to grab her clothes and find Falov.

When she was on her knees, she was greeted with a pair of black boots. As she craned her neck up, Falov stood there with his arms crossed and her clothes hooked in his hand.

"I need your help." The words were bitter on her tongue.

There was a lick of hesitation in his gaze. He clenched his jaw as he looked behind him as if checking no one was nearby. His composure subtly transformed to ease.

"What is it?"

She pointed behind her. "You can't let that ship hit the reefs."

"There's nothing we can do. It's going too fast to stop."

"Not if you can control water."

His eyes hardened, those blue eyes turning to stone. "I can't control anything."

"Bullshit," she spat. "You can help, and we don't have time for you to throw a tantrum. You know how much those reefs mean to my kind."

Her gut twisted when he didn't seem too eager to jump in and offer her a hand. Time was slipping. If he didn't make a decision fast, she would have to do it alone.

"It's where our souls rest, Falov. Getting Nyphadora's heart back won't matter if where it will drift to is gone," her words were hurried, her voice cracking at the end.

Something in her words or her expression must have convinced him because he tightened the leather band in his hair.

"Fine," he grunted.

Without missing a beat, she explained her plan. "We're going to create a whirlpool. When the ship gets caught in it, we'll spit it back out once it faces the other direction."

"That's risky."

"It's all I have," she begged, and she hated the desperation in her voice. They stared at each other, and she watched the bob of his throat.

"Let's go," he relented.

She didn't think twice before she was back in the water, a loud splash following behind her. Facing Falov, she saw the bubble he created around his head, allowing him to breathe. The first time he did it, Syrena froze, open-mouthed and impressed. Even without a tail and webbed hands, he moved through the water seamlessly like the seafolk. They explored together, and as they did, Syrena's heart began to fall for him. It was stupid and naïve, but Falov had a gravitational pull that Syrena hadn't been able to fight.

He talked about his powers with her. He told her how his mother was born under the sea, but gave up that life for his father on land. He spoke about how he promised his mother to never tell a soul about the small dose of power that coursed through him and how—only with her—he wanted to speak openly about it for the first time in his life. Those few months had been magical. Then, it came to an abrupt end just over a year ago when last year's Undertaking began.

"What do I do?" His words sounded muffled behind the bubble. His willingness to help caused her feelings for him to resurface—but then she would think about Nyphadora and be reminded about why she hated him.

"Move the water in the opposite direction as me."

She didn't give him a chance to ask questions. The oncoming ship was close and too large to make a sharp turn like *The Dark Destiny*. She had no doubt they were oblivious to where they were heading and how shallow the water was. If they didn't act soon, the Rafa Reefs would be demolished.

Syrena swam, letting the water coat her skin and use her as a guide. It followed behind her as she yanked on it. She didn't know how Falov was doing, but she hoped he had enough power to cause a strong enough current.

There was panic settling in. The Rafa Reefs could not be ruined. It could not be her fault. She couldn't have the weight of it on her shoulders. She would never be able to face her family again. She would never be able to give her friend the proper sendoff.

Then she felt the tension build as her body was pushed. The swirl was large, the power of the whirlpool taking her wide. She practically cried tears of joy, savoring the power of the sea, thanking Skarb for his great gift. Mermaids praised Skarb for his creation of the undersea, a beautiful world safely built for the seafolk to survive.

Then, a new panic began to set in.

Falov.

She rode the whirlpool in hopes of crashing into him before the ship got caught in the maelstrom. It would be dangerous for him.

Yet, she still hadn't bumped into him.

Syrena dove deeper into the water until she was beneath the whirlpool. The force at which it moved was beautiful, but the ship would be caught in its net soon. She kept her eyes out for a body. It was hard to detect between the ribbons of seaweed and other sea animals, but as she began to lose hope, there he was.

He was conscious at least, but the way he tried to swim out of the swirl showed how tired he was. That bubble would soon be gone, and he would drown.

A part of her hesitated. Wasn't this what she wanted? With him dead, he could never win the emerald Heart, and she could steal Nyphadora's heart from the ship and go home.

She swore at herself as she realized she couldn't leave him. That gravitational pull was still strong, and she let it guide her to him.

She flipped her tail with fervor as she raced towards him. Once she was back in the whirlpool, she swam up to him and grabbed him underneath his arms. His first instinct was to kick the mermaid snatching at him, and she hissed when he hit her stomach.

"It's me, you bastard."

"Don't sneak up on me," he growled.

At that moment, she considered letting him go. "I'm saving your damn life. It's more than you deserve."

The opposing ship was spinning within the whirlpool they created, swirling round and round. The ship was beginning to break under the pressure of movement.

She let Falov go and gave him one last shove, singing to ensure he didn't turn around and stop her. "Start swimming up."

Syrena was back inside the whirlpool, gritting her teeth as she slowed the water down. She needed to time this correctly so the ship would end up pointing in the direction away from the reef. She and the ship spun together, until finally the whirlpool began to dissipate, and the ship was facing the opposite direction. With one last push of the water, Syrena sent the ship sailing away.

Syrena looked in Falov's direction, and he was still swimming up, his bubble now completely gone. Syrena muttered under her breath and grabbed him again. When they broke the surface of the water, Falov took a deep breath in, gasping loudly. He coughed out water, his face turning beet-red as he pulled air into his lungs. Her hands reached out to help, but she seized them back, remembering herself.

"That is the only time I save you. A favor for helping me. Next time, I'll leave you for the seafolk to find your corpse."

She was climbing up onto *The Dark Destiny* before he could bother with a retort.

Six

The next morning was met with tired faces and cloudy skies. Humidity coated her skin like a second pair of clothes. Rain would be upon them soon.

After they returned, Falov immediately ran to the deck where they were greeted with the sight of injured crew members—only small gashes and broken bones, luckily. Luga bounded across the deck like a lost dog, trying to be useful.

Instead of sleeping, Falov ordered Syrena and Luga to count their inventory. Some of their stash had been harmed, but most of it survived the attack. Before she headed to the hold—where she discovered there was a small prison cell—she heard murmurings from the crew about the whirlpool they witnessed. They breathed in relief that their ship hadn't been caught in its clutches.

Syrena didn't feel guilty about what she'd done to the crew. They could handle some danger, especially since they had no qualms with murder.

An unintentional positive: they now had no one on their backs. They could search the reefs peacefully. Well...as long as none of the seafolk saw them and decided they wanted to feast on human legs.

They had anchored the ship, and Falov was speaking with Captain Druz, determining their strategy. It was strange to watch him work the ship. When Syrena had met him, she knew his father was a pirate captain and that Falov had spent his childhood on the sea, but she had never seen him in action. Back then, every moment together was spent either exploring his town, the sea, or each other's bodies.

A voice boomed, and she realized it was Falov. The dominance he displayed was so foreign. With her, he had been soft and gentle. His eyes always peeled for whatever he could imprint into his sketchbook. It had only been a day—an eventful one at that—yet she still hadn't seen him with a sketchbook in his hand. That didn't settle well with her.

"We have two rowboats. Myself and Syrena are in one. Mora and Wysp in the other. We want to keep the group small in case the seafolk strike."

Syrena could see the tension rolling off of Lina, but she kept her mouth shut. Lina understood her place, then—or at least she wouldn't dare question the Captain's nephew and clear successor.

Syrena braided her hair as the rest of the crew chatted logistics and plans, giving her a moment to look out towards the reef. She didn't sense the seafolk, just sea animals lazily swimming around. More importantly, she could tell the Heart wasn't here. The thrum of the emerald gemstone didn't pulse to her. It would be a disappointing day for the crew, but she would waste the time with them.

Approaching the rowboats, Falov gave Syrena an assessing glare, as if checking she was okay. She didn't like his eyes on her. *He* was the one who had been vulnerable yesterday.

"We should go before the sharks start looking for their breakfast," Syrena said, her morning voice rough.

"At least they would leave you alone, right?"

The crew milled around them, so she didn't understand why he openly admitted something that would reveal her as a mermaid. "Exactly. I heard they like men more. Something to do with that extra appendage."

"Who knew those that grace the seas had so much in common?" Falov winked, and she hated that her face heated.

"Maybe I should have eaten you when I had the chance," she muttered under her breath.

"So there is history here, then?" Lina's voice dragged upwards as she headed their way.

Falov blinked, surprised by her intrusion. Did he forget they were on a ship with a full crew? He was acting recklessly, and it would get both of them in trouble. Well...more so him. Syrena could just jump in the water and leave. She tapped her pocket, checking the shell was there, and Lina tracked the movement. Syrena flashed her teeth menacingly, and Lina rolled her eyes.

They stepped apart from each other, and Falov turned to the source of accusation. "We've bumped into each other across town before."

"I can see that there was a lot of bumping."

"Lina," he warned.

"What?" she asked innocently. "I just want to make sure you're being safe."

"I can take care of myself."

Lina grabbed his chin and pouted. "Of course you can. You're no longer a little boy. But she worries me."

"Syrena is no one to worry about," he reassured Lina, but Syrena didn't like how easily he brushed off her capacity for danger.

"Find me something pretty?" Lina asked.

"You know I can't take anything from the reefs."

"Fine, let me ask Mora then."

Falov looked ready to stop her, but he let her go. Syrena had her arms around herself.

"Why is she so obsessed with collecting things from the sea?"

Falov shrugged. "Like most of the crew, she grew up with nothing. Now that she's in a better place, she likes being surrounded by stuff."

"The reefs are sacred," Syrena explained. "Trying to steal anything from there would be seen as cause for death by the seafolk."

"I'm aware."

"I don't even know how she got that necklace." It wasn't impossible that the scales were another mermaid's, but there was a golden chrome in certain lights that resembled Nyphadora's scales. Mermaids shed their scales, and she knew there were landwalkers that traded with the seafolk, so perhaps it was a similar case. At least Syrena tried convincing herself it meant nothing more.

"I've never asked her, but she's a pirate. We're always stumbling across treasure."

"Some would call that stealing."

Falov sighed, as he gestured to the rowboat. "Hop in."

Falov didn't know what came over him last night when he jumped into the water with Syrena. It had been fucking cold and—as one would expect—very wet. He didn't care about the fate of the other ship, but Syrena's fear had been palpable. He understood the importance of the reefs. Syrena had explained it to him back when she actually was willing to have a conversation with him. He missed those days when she was chatty and lively, and he absorbed each of her words like he was a dry sponge. Now, she barely looked at him, and when she did open her mouth, it was like a sharp blade, ready to strike. The reminder of the fact the reefs were their final resting place pierced him deep, especially when coupled with her desperate pleading.

On one side of them was the deepest blue of the dark sea, and on the other was the colorful ecosystem of the reefs. As Falov rowed the boat alongside the shoal, admiring the reef's beauty, he said, "Let me know if you feel anything."

"It's not here. I told you that already," she snapped.

At that moment, he wanted to shake her and tell her why he did what he did. He wasn't the cruel murderer she concocted in her head. But...he tightened his lips together. He didn't need her pushing him over the boat.

"Then at least act like you're searching." He turned his head around where he saw Mora and Wysp slowly making their way around.

Syrena dramatically craned her head over the water, as if looking through the water's surface and into its depths for the Heart.

Settled back into her seat, she said with little enthusiasm, "Nothing."

"You were never such a smartass before."

Syrena stiffened in her spot. It was nice to have the power to ruffle her by mentioning their past. As much as she wanted to act like the cool and collected mermaid, she had an innate passion to her that always seeped out, and those cracks were showing.

"And I never thought you could kill someone."

But, she always circled back to that. It was a truth that disturbed him. He never thought it possible either, but that moment had been fast, and he didn't have a chance to think about the consequences.

"I see something!" Wysp yelled excitedly, the rowboat rocking beneath him.

Falov and Syrena glanced at each other, and for the first time in what felt like years, she held his gaze. Those brown eyes were like the dark sand found on the seafloor. He could search them for hours, seeking treasure—only to realize the treasure was always her.

She turned her attention away to watch as Mora tried to calm Wysp down so the rowboat would stop rocking.

"Should we entertain this?" Falov asked.

Syrena gave a sharp nod, and Falov rowed over to them. Syrena dragged her hand through the water, and it responded by wrapping itself up to her elbow in a liquid rope. Whatever she was doing, he hoped she was careful. He didn't need Mora and Wysp seeing her powers. He gave her the benefit of the doubt that she was just scanning the water below to make sure what Wysp noticed was actually the Heart.

Thankfully, as they neared, Syrena let the water go. It slithered down her arm like a snake. He hoped nothing else would pop out from the water and strike them.

"I see something shiny," Wysp pointed into the depths. His excited demeanor almost had Falov believing he could have spotted the Heart.

Syrena's unimpressed expression reminded him of what she had said. It wasn't here, and this entire mission was just a way for Syrena to build trust with the crew. Although Falov was starting to think she had other motives.

"I can dive down," Falov said as he began unbuttoning his shirt.

"I'll go," Mora chimed in.

"No," Syrena snapped.

It was the latter that made him blink once, then twice. Why did Syrena care if he went down? He would have expected she volunteered him to go get eaten by the seafolk.

"I'll go," Mora repeated, eyeing the both of them suspiciously. "Maybe you two can take the time to work out the weird tension."

"There's no tension," Falov said too quickly to be considered casual, and Wysp looked like he held back a laugh.

Syrena opened her mouth but shut it. She clearly wanted to reveal what he did and who he did it to, but doing so would open a line of questions neither of them would be able to answer without telling the full truth.

Mora narrowed her eyes. "Just keep a close eye out for any seafolk. I don't want to become their dinner."

All of them nodded and Wysp handed her a rod with a net attached. She hesitated to grab it.

"What the fuck do I need this for?"

The man gritted his teeth. "To get the Heart in case it's in a hard place to reach." He shushed Mora before she could speak again and flipped over the rod. The end had been carved into a sharp point. "Perfect for any seafolk who tries anything."

Mora dove into the water, the net in hand.

Wysp shrugged. "It's my good luck net when fishing."

"Let's hope she doesn't break it when she's down there then," Falov said.

They waited, watching Mora swim down into the sea, her body becoming smaller and smaller. He didn't want to lose eyes on her, but he supposed it was good that Syrena was next to him watching closely, too.

What wasn't good...the way she was biting her lip and concentrating very hard.

"What's wrong?"

She didn't respond at first, as if lost in a trance of some kind. He could feel Wysp shifting in his rowboat. Birds squawked from above.

"Do you miss home?" The words were out of Falov's mouth before he could even think. He didn't like how concentrated she had become.

Syrena whipped her head around so fast that her long braid slapped her face. "There's nothing wrong. Now stop bothering me."

Her attention was back on the water, and there was such a strange stillness. The waves lapped slowly, and there was no other life above water. There was not even a cloud in the sky, like even Skarb didn't deign to disturb the peace of the reefs. It made Falov's skin crawl.

Suddenly the water began to rattle, and rings of water bubbled up to the surface around both of the rowboats. Wysp's wide eyes told Falov this wasn't an illusion. Syrena, on the other hand, didn't seem surprised. He was about to question her when Mora burst out of the water.

"Row those fucking oars!" she yelled as she clung to the side of the boat and flopped inside.

Her face was red from exertion, but it was the puncture wounds in her arm that had caught Falov's attention.

Fuck. The seafolk knew they were here.

His muscles flexed as he tugged on the oars to get the boat moving. Wysp did the same. He didn't focus on Mora too long, but he could see her energy wane. She needed help, but they couldn't give it out here.

He wanted to ask Syrena to hold them off, to do *something*, but he doubted she would when he suspected she had been the one who alerted them to their presence in the first place.

She was so pissed at him that she was willing to let innocent lives get caught in the crossfire of whatever was going on between them. He should have never allowed her to stay on the damned ship.

His arms ached with each row, but he wouldn't stop. Even the sea breeze wasn't enough to stop the sweat that rolled down his forehead and back. Wysp looked even worse, and Falov could tell he was slowing down.

"They're surrounding us," Mora warned from the spot where she was cradling her arm and using a strip of her shirt that she ripped to staunch the flow of blood.

Falov glanced about to see that swarms of mermaids were, in fact, all around them. They would soon start jumping out of the water and clawing at them.

"Syrena," his voice cracked. He didn't care about his pride right now. She needed to do something.

She cocked her head to the right, her eyes innocent-looking as she fluttered her lashes.

"Are you scared?" she whispered as she lithely moved towards him on the small boat. Her fingers dragged across his chin and down his neck.

He didn't stop rowing though. She wouldn't intimidate him.

"I'm sure Wysp and Mora are scared. Just like Nyphadora must have felt when you cornered her and took her life, then had the audacity to steal her heart." She poked at his chest, her finger digging deep.

"You can end this."

"What if I never want this to end?"

A piercing scream sounded from the other rowboat, and Falov only caught a glimpse of Wysp being dragged into the water by scaled arms. Mora was fighting off a mermaid with claws that were wrapped around her neck. She was reaching for the stupid net, but it was too far for her to reach.

"Please," he begged. "They don't deserve this. If anyone dies today, it should be me."

Syrena chuckled, the sound cold and dead, like she didn't care either way. She just wanted revenge, and deep down, Falov couldn't even blame her.

"Tell them to let the other two go and take me." It was the only thing he could offer.

"Falov!" Mora shrieked.

That sound would haunt him for the rest of his life. This was all his fault. He should have never used Nyphadora's heart to enter the Undertaking, but if it hadn't been hers, Captain Druz or Lina would have killed a different mermaid.

Falov shook his head and prepared to go after his shipmates, when everything paused as Syrena's lips pressed together. He couldn't hear anything, but it was as if the song of the wind blew by, stilling the world around them. The mermaid attacking Mora nodded at Syrena and dove back in the water. He watched in awe as the chaos turned to calm, and so quickly back to disaster, when Wysp was heaved out of the water and thrown on the rowboat.

Then, all he heard was screaming.

Seven

Syrena watched as Falov lifted Wysp up to *The Dark Destiny*. Mora was on their heels climbing up the ladder silently, except for hisses of pain. In addition to the wound on her arm, she now sported a bruise on her eye and scratches across her face. Yet it was nothing in comparison to Wysp. His arm hung at an awkward angle, and his shirt was completely tattered, revealing every spot the mermaids had dug their claws and teeth. He would need a healer and a long recovery.

When Syrena hopped over the rail, she and Falov were swarmed by the crew. They hounded Falov with questions, while others carried Wysp and Mora down into the belly of the ship. Lina had been the first by Mora's side, wiping Mora's wet hair from her face and whispering words Syrena couldn't hear. Through the chaos, Syrena barely felt the cold raindrops splattering on her skin.

It was a strange sight to see how quickly everyone stepped in to provide whatever help they could.

It was even stranger when she felt a stab of guilt—slight but still evident—in her chest. She didn't know what to make of it, but while everyone took care of each other, Syrena disappeared to Falov's quarters to get away.

But before she could get very far, she was being yanked and thrown into a small, dark room. A quick sizzle and flick, and there was a low light burning. Syrena blinked, her eyes adjusting to the darkness, and she wished she could blow out the oil lamp.

Falov looked ready to tear her apart

He was breathing deeply, his blue eyes raging like a violent sea.

"You bitch," he hissed.

She let the shock of the moment wash away before her eyes landed directly on him. Coolly, she said. "I have no idea what you're angry about."

He stared at her as if scouring his mind for how he wanted to kill her. She licked her lips, preparing herself, but his eyes quickly darted to her mouth and lingered. Her body grew taut in anticipation, like muscle memory took over. Perhaps, this could end differently—anything to take her mind off of the regret—but then his anger returned.

"*You* brought the attack on us. *You* almost had Mora and Wysp killed because of a petty fight between us."

Syrena's mouth hung open. "Petty? You think the murder of my friend is a petty motive for trying to sabotage this foolish mission?"

"No," he pulled back sharply, his warmth leaving her space. He clawed his fingers through his damp hair, hissing as they tangled in the long strands. "No," he repeated. "I'm angry at myself. I should have never let you on this ship."

Syrena scoffed. "Without me, you would have no chance."

"Mora would have navigated us in the right direction. She still will."

"You have such faith in your crew." Although the seafolk were a bloodthirsty species and they liked to keep that illusion alive to the landwalkers, they also had the same sense of protection for their kin. Her large family always took care of each other, and Nyphadora and her never let each other stray too far. Well...excluding that one day.

"Trust is the most essential component of any crew."

"Yet you lie to them about me."

He ducked his head. She knew he was ashamed as he said, "It'll help us find the Heart."

"Why do you want the Heart so desperately?"

There was a blip of hesitation that came from him, as if he had more than one reason for his desire. He seemed to finally decide on one as he replied, "I don't know what lies you all spout to make us landwalkers look like enemies, but we will all die, Syrena. The court will be flooded over by the sea because its power will not be replenished. The Weather Gods punish us for failing, and the seafolk will perish along with us."

"I'm not asking why landwalkers seek the Heart each year. Why do *you* want the Heart?" she prodded.

Falov stayed quiet, and in the silence the room seemed to close in on them. It was as if whatever Falov carried sucked the air from the room and squeezed it tight.

It brought Syrena back to a time when she visited him on land. It was one of the last times before catastrophe struck their lives. Falov was drinking at a tavern, and when she walked in, his eyes bore into her. Her dress was the same teal as the ends of her hair, but the top layer was made of netting, giving her the appearance she had been caught. It was Nyphadora's dress, one she had used to seduce a landwalker a few years ago. She and Nyphadora had been getting ready together when Syrena told her friend who she was going to see.

Nyphadora had smirked at her, "It's becoming serious between the two of you."

Syrena had blushed. "He makes me feel special. In our world where it's so easy to get lost—even as a princess—I feel *seen*. I'm not just another body for reproduction or another political maneuver to build allyship. With him, I'm just Syrena."

Nyphadora had momentarily hung her head, as if she were sad, but after a moment her smile returned. "I know that feeling. Never let it go."

Then, Syrena remembered Nyphadora kissing her on the cheek and telling her to seduce Falov to his knees.

Syrena understood why Falov had fallen so easily into her trap. The dress clung to Syrena's chest and hips tightly, accentuating the strong body she needed to maneuver through the sea.

Falov had walked up to her and claimed her lips. The whole tavern was staring, but Syrena didn't care as she moaned into his mouth. It was exhilarating being watched as Falov explored her body with his large hands, cupping one of her breasts and pinching the nipple peaked beneath the netting. The whole exchange lasted less than a minute, but she remembered feeling like she couldn't breathe unless he gave her his breath.

Syrena cleared her throat, bringing herself back to the present. Falov eyed her warily, but she waited, still expecting him to respond. And a deep part of her that was lost in that memory was expecting this moment to turn to something more, to go back to the easiness of the past where they could fall together like they were each other's own safety nets.

"Like you said, I'm nobody to you." He cleared his throat. "You're no longer owed my story, Syrena. Just like I'm not owed yours."

And then he blew out the oil lamp and left her alone in the cold dark.

Falov returned to his crew—the people who reminded him of exactly why this Undertaking mattered. The people who dedicated their lives to his father and now his uncle.

"How are they doing?" he asked Lina who sat like a guard, back ramrod straight, her eyes open and focused on the two patients who slept peacefully. Their bodies were both covered in bandages, and the guilt he felt at causing their pain scraped at his insides.

Lina didn't take her eyes off either of them. "They'll live."

Nothing more and nothing less. For Lina, as long as the person was breathing, she didn't care how much pain they were in. It was a reality of being a pirate. So many crew members faced danger and made it out alive, but were forever changed by injuries inflicted on them. A risk each of them accepted when they boarded a ship.

"What happened out there?" The words came out sharp, like Lina's tongue was made of steel.

It was the question Falov had been waiting for ever since they'd returned. In the stress of ensuring Wysp and Mora survived, Captain Druz must have stalled on asking. Falov should probably go to him and explain, but he was tired.

"We were ambushed," Falov simply said, but that wasn't enough for Lina.

"You should have been protecting them."

"I was prepared to die if needed," Falov growled.

"And yet, there is barely a scratch on your body." She assessed him. "Or Syrena's."

"What are you suggesting?"

"That you were too focused on making gooey eyes at her instead of watching *your* crew."

Falov ground his teeth because her accusation was right, but for the wrong reason. He'd had his eyes on Syrena because she had been the cause of the attack, and had been their only way out of it.

"It's not my crew yet," Falov mumbled, trying to excuse his poor actions.

Lina gave an exasperated sigh and shook her head. "Falov, whether you earned it or not, you're going to be captain soon. And as captain, your crew always comes first. A girl cannot stand in the way of that."

"Is that what happened to you?"

Lina flinched in her seat, her fingers immediately finding the scales around her neck.

He nodded at the jewelry. "Did you pick this ship over who gave those to you?"

"Who gave me these doesn't matter. It never would have worked. *The Dark Destiny* is my home, and only death will separate us." And although those words were meant to come out cold, as a way to show her strength, they left her lips like a somber fog.

"It's okay to admit you miss them."

The sheen in her eyes caused Falov to freeze, as if any movement would shake Lina out of whatever trance she was in. Perhaps seeing Mora injured stirred something in her. "She would have given it all up for me. She wanted to find a home more inland, away from the sea, so that she wouldn't be reminded where she came from," Lina said.

It was rare for a relationship between the seafolk and landwalkers to work. First, it required pushing aside all the hatred between the two species. Even if they did, there were negative connotations behind such unions—so much so that many mermaids gave up their tails to avoid it.

When Syrena and he were spending more and more time together, he had thought about whether she would ever give up her tail to be with him. When he discovered she was a princess of one of the territories below, he stopped entertaining the idea. She couldn't, and he learned she never would because of how much she loved the sea. It was her home.

So Falov convinced himself it would have been different for him and Syrena. He could join her for short stints in the sea, unlike other landwalkers, and she could spend days at a time by his side as a landwalker. But he supposed none of it mattered anymore.

"I couldn't give up the life on this ship for her," Lina admitted.

She wiped her eyes. He had never seen her like this before. Open and vulnerable. Perhaps being faced with the possibility of death surrounding them reminded her of the fragility of their lives.

"*The Dark Destiny* appreciates your service."

"Does it?" she bit out, but before he could push her on it, small heaves sounded from the hall, and Falov smiled as Luga popped inside the room with a bucket of water in each hand.

His face was beet red, and out of generosity, Falov grabbed them from him before they spilled all over the floor.

Luga bent over, his hands on his knees. "Here's. The. Water." Each word came out after a deep breath.

"Great," Lina proclaimed. "Now you can wash our patients' feet."

Luga's mouth turned to disgust as he looked at the sand that clung to their skin. "But—"

"No buts. Wysp and Mora depend on you."

Those words seemed to churn something inside him, as if he was reminded of his role and responsibility as cabin boy. Like he was reminded of the honor of it.

He saluted Lina and Falov, then got to work.

Falov shook his head, chuckling at the enthusiasm. Just like when Falov was young, Luga wanted to prove himself.

"I think it's time for a drink," Falov announced.

Lina didn't object as she left their bedsides, and went to the deck. Before Falov joined her, he stopped in front of his quarters, where the door was shut. He thought about inviting Syrena to express his gratitude for her having ultimately saved his friends. Yet...anger bubbled up again, and he couldn't.

Instead, he spent the rest of the night drinking. And when the crew went to bed, he laid down on the deck to fall asleep beneath the stars.

Eight

The next morning everything was back to normal. Pirates didn't allow tragedy to cloud their jobs, especially when they were on an expedition. The sea wouldn't patiently wait for them to recover, so they adjusted and moved on fast.

It meant Mora was back in action, and livelier than ever. Apparently, her deep unconsciousness had brought her vivid dreams. She didn't have the Sight since she wasn't the minister of the Rain Court, but it didn't stop her from believing her dream was prophetic.

Falov remembered how his stepfather would come down in the morning chanting prayers, speaking words of damnation, or praising the Gods. Over the years, Falov had learned there were multiple landwalkers who could qualify as a minister—since more than one person had the Sight at a time. When a minister died, the next was chosen by accomplishing tests his stepfather wouldn't divulge to him. The whole order of the ministers seemed cultish to him, but his stepfather had been nice enough, so Falov never pried.

Wysp had told Falov that he'd woken up during the night with Mora mumbling jumbled words in her sleep. They both laughed, but Falov avoided glancing too long at the bloody bandages covering most of his body.

Everyone's attention was on Mora now. She wouldn't let it go, even after Lina tried explaining numerous times she should use other navigation techniques that were more tangible than her dreams, instead. Mora wouldn't have it.

The crew circled her. Even Captain Druz listened closely as she rambled on about how the ship had flown in the sky because a pod of dolphins gave it powers to do so. Falov had to stop himself from rolling his eyes because as crazy as her dream was, he still felt responsible for what had happened to her yesterday.

Captain Druz and Falov had a quick exchange that morning which had left him questioning everything. It had been one question, but Falov's response haunted him.

His uncle had clasped his shoulder. "Do you have something to tell me?"

Falov had hesitated, but he swallowed the lump in his throat and shook his head. "No. Yesterday was unfortunate, but we have a goal. We can't linger on the past."

Captain Druz's eyes had shone with disappointment, but he had let Falov go.

When Mora's story turned to magical birds who spoke to her, Falov assessed the group, noting one missing figure. Perhaps Syrena decided to dive off the ship and abandon them after all. He wouldn't blame her. Honestly, a part of him would have been relieved. There were too many emotions between them, and Falov didn't know how to navigate those depths. Lina had made a good point last night. If he was to inherit *The Dark Destiny*, then he would have to let Syrena go.

"Anyways," Mora said. "All that to say, the birds told me to go to Balkov Island."

Chatter immediately erupted as everyone began discussing the suggestion, and how they felt about the idea. Captain Druz adjusted his hat, letting the information settle. He, no doubt, was thinking strategically about the matter. This wouldn't be a place they could jump into. This was a home to many people, one strongly protected. They would need permission to get inside the guarded island.

"That's an insane idea," a familiar voice commented from behind him. He hated how quickly he turned around to look at her.

"No one asked for your opinion," Lina responded, annoyed.

"I was allowed on this ship as a second opinion because of my amazing tracking abilities." Syrena flicked her hair behind her shoulders, the long strands nearly smacking Falov in the face. "And my opinion is that it's a bad idea. The Balkovians hate pirates."

"The feeling's mutual," a crew member who stood behind Falov coughed into the back of his hand. The Balkovians were a group of landwalkers who had left the mainland in protest of the Undertaking. There was no representative team from the island competing in the Undertaking, and pirates disparaged them for their cowardice.

"Which means they'll hate you, too, when we show up," Lina shot back at Syrena, as if trying to snare her in a lie. Syrena didn't take the bait.

"I'm trying to warn you. If you thought yesterday was bad, then this whole ship will be in flames before we get anywhere near Balkov Island. They show no mercy."

"And mermaids do?" It was Wysp this time who spoke. He clearly was still shaken up from yesterday, and he had to lean on the ship's railing to remain upright.

"Mermaids are a different species," Syrena explained. "It's in—" she stopped, as if she were about to misspeak. "It's in their nature to want to abolish any threats."

Mora finally stepped in again. "I think this is the best route we have. Unless, of course, you have something better, Syrena."

Syrena bit her lip. She was back to square one. The crew didn't trust her because she had returned unscathed like Falov. This was an opportunity for them both to show their dedication to the crew, and to winning this Undertaking.

"We'll go," Falov finally said. Captain Druz almost looked shocked by his declaration but did not refute his nephew's decree. "But it will just be me and Syrena who venture to the island. The rest of you will stay and guard the ship."

Objections started immediately, but the only person he had his eyes on was Syrena. She looked both pleased and annoyed, understanding it was the strategic call, but hating that she would need to spend even more time with him. He didn't care. After what she had done yesterday, he would use Syrena's gifts for good. Her siren song would get them inside easily.

"If that's decided," Captain Druz's voice boomed, "then we sail for Balkov Island."

It took them five days to reach Balkov Island. The large stone gate that surrounded the whole island was a familiar sight. It was a protection against other landwalkers. However, as a mermaid, Syrena knew that the seafolk could easily enter and exit through underwater tunnels, because she had visited the island as a royal representative for her people. Her parents kept a strong alliance with the Balkovians, and Syrena never missed the opportunity to explore somewhere new. What hid behind the large wall was an immaculate sight.

"Keep vigilant. Even if they are hospitable, you must keep one eye open at all times. I've heard nightmares about the torture they cause to pirates," Captain Druz warned them both,, but she barely paid attention. Her eyes were fixated on the fortress ahead. "Did you hear me, Syrena?"

She didn't turn her head to the Captain, but nodded once.

"I don't know who you are or where you came from, but this is a serious matter."

The chiding tone finally drew her attention to the old Captain.

"Falov will protect you," he said.

She crossed her arms and smiled. "I'll be the one protecting him."

Falov coughed, but Captain Druz looked slightly impressed.

"Don't do anything reckless."

With those parting words, Syrena and Falov's rowboat was lowered to the sea. They brought very little: a change of clothes, some coin, and their prayers to Skarb that they would make it out alive.

"You don't have to look so angry," Falov commented from where he sat opposite of her.

"How am I supposed to look?"

"Scared."

"Why would I need to be scared?"

"Because we are heading into enemy territory."

Syrena scoffed. "I am not their enemy. *You* are."

A deep sigh showed his exasperation. "Yet the plan was to act as a newly married couple who have been lost at sea after a storm."

Syrena didn't want to think about the inane plan the crew of *The Dark Destiny* had concocted. How Syrena was busily helping Luga wash the deck, sweating on her hands and knees when Lina, Mora, and Falov all came to explain how this would work.

That night, Falov had added that she would need to use her powers to lure whatever guards were stationed to allow them passage onto the island.

She had been expecting the request from him. A part of her had wanted to spit in his face and tell him to find another way, but what he had said struck something deep inside of her.

You're no longer owed my story, Syrena. Just like I'm not owed yours.

Months ago, they had been so open and honest with each other. Now, at times, she felt like Falov was a stranger. She didn't understand his heart anymore, because nothing she could even dream of could justify what he had done.

The shadow of the gate eclipsed them as they neared. She just hoped this visit would be quick.

Syrena sensed exactly where the guards were, and she narrowed her eyes at them.

"Maybe you should cover your ears."

"Your music never impacted me before."

"I didn't hate you then," she quipped, before letting the tune trail its way over to listening ears. Thankfully, Falov put the oars down and did as she suggested.

It didn't take long before she heard the hinges of the gate squeak. Syrena clocked the exact moment Falov got his first peek of paradise. He gasped, and it was a noise she had never heard from him—such a sound of wonder. His hand twitched, and she could tell he wanted to draw the sight before him.

It was like a different world on the other side of the gate. While Falov's home was cold and harsh with its stone buildings and strong reinforcements against the constant rain, Balkovians appreciated the water and let the natural element center their home. Even the sky seemed a shade brighter above the island.

White sand glittered like gems had been crushed into dust. Everyone was dressed in almost nothing, splashing in the water, savoring the healing properties of the gift from the Weather Gods.

Syrena craned her neck to spy the terracotta castle standing in the distance. The structure was a gift from the Thunder Court, reinforced to withstand torrential downpours.

She let Falov row them all the way to the shore so she could avoid wetting her necklace, which was safely around her neck. It wasn't like she needed to hide her identity here. Everyone would recognize her, but she didn't want to be a flailing mermaid right now.

"Princess Syrena!" a cheery voice exclaimed.

Falov turned so fast in her direction, she feared he would fall over. "You didn't tell me they knew who you were?"

She fluttered her lashes at him. "I am a frequent visitor of Balkov Island."

"So why didn't you say anything when we agreed to the plan?"

"Because I like to be a nuisance. Also, you told me to lure our way in. What easier way to get us inside than to sing about an old friend coming to visit?"

"You're going to get us killed."

She stepped up to him and flicked his nose. "Not us. *You.*"

"I thought we were over this."

"Just because I decided to save Wysp and Mora doesn't mean I accomplished what I needed with you."

He opened his mouth to speak but the figure that had welcomed them was now approaching with open arms.

King Pasek wrapped Syrena in a warm embrace, and she could sense Falov stiffen.

"A beauty returns to us!" King Pasek marvelled as he stroked the ends of her hair. Syrena leaned in close, delighting in the tension she could feel rolling off Falov.

"You know I find it hard to stay away from the pleasure of your company."

King Pasek laughed, bumping his shoulder with hers. "You flatter me."

Deciding to show some mercy to Falov—who she glimpsed to be ready to strike the King if she kept flirting—Syrena asked, "Where is your husband?"

The King tsked. "You know him, he's like a house cat. He's just waking up from a nap." That bright smile dimmed when he finally turned to Falov, assessing a potential threat.

"Who is your guest?"

Syrena glanced over at Falov who now looked nervous. This could be her opportunity to end him like she always planned. All she had to do was reveal him as a pirate, and the Balkovians would not hesitate to kill him. It was so easy. An opportunity gifted from Skarb.

So she wasn't prepared for the words leaving her lips.

"My husband."

Nine

*H*er *husband*, Falov kept repeating in his head. Falov wondered why he had agreed with Mora's plan. Knowing Syrena had a close bond with the Balkovian royals left this mission on rocky waters. Any second she could decide to betray him, leaving him to drown.

Falov's feet kept sinking into the sand. King Pasek—a dark-skinned man who bested Falov in height—walked gracefully across the shore. Even Syrena showed no signs of struggle as she strode side-by-side with the King, talking animatedly with him. If he didn't know the King was married, Falov would think Syrena was flirting to get under Falov's skin. Though, something told him marriage might not stop her from doing just that.

His inability to traverse the beach caused him to stray behind, flanked by three guards who had their eyes pinned to him, as if waiting for him to do something troublesome. If they would have been smarter, they would've kept their attention on Syrena.

"Husband, I woke up in a fright when you weren't in bed beside me," a deeply lush voice sounded from the stairs.

Falov turned his eyes upwards to find a man wearing a long robe. He flitted down the stairs with beautiful purple fabric trailing behind him.

"I had Kingly duties to attend to, my love," King Pasek sighed, but Falov barely heard it because of how loud Syrena became.

"Marius!" Syrena shouted as she ran up to him, and pecked a kiss directly on the man's bald head. "I missed you."

"Princess Syrena," he pulled her away from him so he could inspect her. "It's been so long, and you show up looking like shit."

The man touched Syrena's billowy, white shirt—which was clean, but the fabric was not as lavish as the Balkovians liked to dress. Falov looked down at himself, cringing at the compared quality of his clothes.

"You look like shit, too, sweet boy," Marius pointed out, and Falov had to sink the urge to shrink into himself as all the room's attention turned to him. "Oh, but you have those charming eyes to make up for it. No wonder you married him."

Falov reddened at the compliment.

"He is a sweet boy, isn't he?" Syrena joked along, but he could see the tension in her jaw.

"You must be hungry." King Pasek said as he approached Marius and Syrena. Once again, Falov was forgotten.

"Starving," Syrena nodded.

"As much as we love the seafolk, the way you eat down there is...questionable," Marius commented. Falov had to agree. The first time Falov swam in the sea with Syrena, he watched as the seafolk caught fish with their bare hands and bit directly into them. Even Syrena didn't have the stomach for that, she had confessed.

"You're just picky," Syrena poked the consort's slightly exposed chest.

He grabbed her finger. "Good thing dinner is almost ready."

"Indeed," King Pasek agreed.

"But you must both change first. We cannot allow such filth at our table."

Syrena clapped. "I can't wait to see what you have for me today."

Marius dipped down to whisper in Syrena's ear, but he spoke loud enough for everyone to hear. "Something that will bring your husband to his knees."

Falov gulped as he watched Syrena and Marius leave.

The King and his consort's room was as grand as the rest of their home, but it did not make sense to Syrena one bit.

It was a large, circular room at the highest level of the castle. Their bed was made of a springy net that bounced when weight pressed upon it. She could not imagine it was comfortable, even if it was big enough to fit more than ten people on it. Under the bed was a large pool that housed a dazzling array of saltwater fish. There were no windows, because all the walls were exposed to the elements. From this high up, she had a beautiful view of the sea. Luckily, there was a roof over their heads, because she would rather not fight the rainstorm that had begun as she was getting ready. Though she had no doubt that the roof could be removed whenever the weather called for it. It was why Marius had begun to develop sun spots on his light skin.

The patter of the raindrops provided a calming ambience, and she breathed in the fresh, petrichor smell.

"Don't just stand there," Marius said as he passed by her to walk into the closet. Syrena peeked inside the room—almost as big as the one she stood in—filled to its brim with clothes. With how little clothes the Balkovians wore, she was always shocked the royals had so many. "Tell me about that pretty husband of yours."

Syrena ducked her head, growing shy.

"I am upset I was not invited to the wedding, by the way." Marius pouted.

She joined him in the closet. "There was no wedding to attend." Syrena shrugged. "It was a private affair." An easy lie, though in the back of her head, she was reminded of the conversation they once had, how Falov wanted to celebrate whatever love he found in silence. He didn't need an audience. Syrena, at that time, had disagreed. Mermaids liked to boast about their accomplishments, and Syrena was no different. When her oldest sister was married, she had a lavish wedding. One Syrena had desired herself. As Falov and Syrena spent more time together, though, her opinion had changed.

"Well, tell me about him. What's your story?" Marius planted his hands on his hips as he inspected two items of clothing.

Syrena, unable to stand still, walked on, dragging her fingers through all the luxurious fabrics.

"He—" It was strange to have to speak about him affectionately again. For months, her thoughts surrounding him had been nothing but hatred, dreaming about his downfall. But she had to set that aside if she wanted to get Nyphadora's heart back. "He's special, a quiet observer, able to scout a room so quickly and tell you exactly how many people are in there and if they are a threat. I think that makes him the skilled artist he is.

"When I met him, he seemed lonely. Though, I would later learn he had a family—they just weren't blood. He loves them deeply. I think a part of him constantly worries he will lose them, forcing him to do what he doesn't truly want." Syrena thought back to the times he had voiced to her how becoming captain was a destiny he dreaded, and how he hoped his father lived a long life, so he wouldn't have to take over anytime soon.

Syrena continued. "That initial time together was like a dream. I snuck out of the water almost daily. Nyphadora was livid that I wasn't telling her where I was going all the time. Well...until she cornered me and forced it out. After she learned about Falov, she spied on him, and discovered he was an honorable man. She was happy for us," Syrena's voice cracked.

She didn't realize that Marius was so close to her until he placed his hands on her shoulders, comforting her. "I'm sorry to hear that she's gone."

Syrena shook her head, refusing to let her thoughts wander to that pain. She didn't think she could speak kindly about Falov if she did. "Falov and I did everything together. Danced at taverns until my feet blistered, ate foods that you can't find under the sea, talked through the night until the sun was poking through the clouds again."

"Fooled around," Marius joked.

Syrena chuckled, and it felt good to do so. Strange, too, to have it be because she was talking about Falov.

"That, too."

"That sounds beautiful. I can see from the way you radiate when you speak about him that you love him."

The words rocked her because they weren't true. Syrena didn't think she ever loved him. Perhaps she would have gotten there in time.

"It was simple and so different from the courting I grew up expecting."

"Do your parents approve?"

"They…" Falov had met them once. It wasn't intentional, but while the two of them were exploring the sea together, her mother had caught them. As soon as she had, her father popped out as well. "They are intrigued by him."

An understatement. When they discovered he was a landwalker with powers—something that had become rare—they welcomed him with open arms. Syrena kept the fact he was a pirate out of it, though she doubted they hadn't figured it out with their own sleuthing.

Marius hummed. "This conversation only confirmed one thing: less is more with him."

Then, he showed her what she would be wearing for dinner, and she laughed—fully laughed. This would be a different kind of torture than Captain Druz had warned them about.

Ten

Falov spent an hour with King Pasek, who prodded him with constant questions, leaving Falov with barely a second to breathe. Then, when he thought he was safe from being forced to adhere to the Balkovian's fashion, a servant handed him a cloth. One *piece* of cloth.

King Pasek chuckled, likely at Falov's worried expression.

"Let's see what's hiding under those layers."

So now Falov was heading to dinner dressed in a scant fabric barely big enough to cover his groin. Only a golden brooch shaped like a fish held it together at his hip. He had to constantly fight the urge to cover himself with his hands.

"Dinner is just in this room," a servant said as they directed Falov.

Falov nodded, dismissing the servant. Before going inside, Falov collected himself. In the rush of introductions and questions, Falov barely had a moment to remember he was in enemy territory. One wrong slip of the mouth, and he would find himself on the wrong end of a blade. He didn't think being married to Syrena would be enough to save him.

Falov rubbed at his face, taking one last breath before deciding to enter when he heard soft footsteps approaching.

Turning towards the source, Falov almost tripped over himself.

Syrena stood there like a true princess of the sea. He homed in on her, unable to look anywhere else. Her long skirt reflected in the moonlight, the white, iridescent fabric reminiscent of her tail. But the length didn't provide any modesty. It clung to her body, accentuating her hips, and the subtle sheerness of it caused his eyes to trail upward until he landed on her top—if he could even call it that. It covered little. It was a collection of pearl chains that draped across her chest, some longer and others shorter, but there was nothing but her bare skin beneath them. Although he had seen her breasts countless times, there was something extra sensual about them being adorned this way. To finish off the look, a crown of pearls sat atop her head, a signal of her status.

He approached Syrena, his hands itching to touch her skin, his mouth anxious to feast on her nipples, which exposed themselves with each step she made.

Syrena put her hand up, and in his desire, his chest collided with her palm.

"This show isn't for you," Syrena whispered. "Not anymore."

Her hand brushed his abdomen as she brought it down, and it left goose bumps. Her own eyes took him in, and he couldn't bear it anymore. He wanted to push her against the wall, to claim her, to drag them back to a past where they were always touching in those intimate moments together.

He heard a clunk coming from the dining room.

Falov shook his head, trying to wash away the lusty mist. "Syrena," was the only thing he was able to get out, his voice so rough it sounded like he'd swallowed sand.

"We should go. It's rude to keep royalty waiting."

Those words shook him back to reality, to whose territory they were in. *Keep it together.* The Dark Destiny *depends on you,* Falov reminded himself.

Falov offered his hand to her; she hesitated. In those seconds, there was an immense amount of guilt wavering over him. This tension, this fallout, was his fault. There was no denying it.

Even while he told her he didn't owe her his story, he wanted to get on his knees and apologize, to explain it all. Would telling her the truth be enough for things to go back to the way they once were?

But then she took his hand, and the moment changed to the next.

They walked into the dining room. Falov had expected extravagance, but the room was quaint and intimate while still reflecting the grandeur of the rest of the castle, with its large crystal chandelier twinkling along the walls, and its accents of gold plated metal. The stone table at its center only seated four.

"Sometimes the occasion calls for privacy, Mr. Falov," King Pasek explained.

Falov nodded, gulping. He felt a squeeze, and his eyes wandered to their conjoined hands and then to Syrena's face—but her attention was on the King.

Marius didn't seem to miss the gesture, but he only pulled out a chair for Syrena. Falov led her over and as she sat, he caught a glimpse of her peaked nipples. His breath hitched, his body growing tight.

Taking his own seat, Falov finally said something. "Thank you both for such great hospitality."

"Anything for our favorite princess."

Syrena waved off the King's kind words. "You flatter me. There are so many princesses in the sea. I barely make the top ten, I'm sure."

That was something Falov learned after spending time with Syrena. Being a princess as a seafolk was not unique. There were so many villages below, and the seafolk reproduced quickly. Syrena was one of eight children. His mother—a former princess of the sea—had twelve other siblings.

Marius poured a glass of something bubbly and bright blue. He handed one glass to Syrena, and another to Falov.

When Falov eyed it suspiciously, Marius said, "It's sparkling wine made with the juice of the lubi flower."

Syrena choked and coughed into her hand, redirecting all the table's attention to her.

Falov anchored his hand on the table, ready to help, but she waved him away.

"What's wrong?" Falov asked worriedly.

King Pasek jumped to answer, "In large quantities, the lubi flower has...interesting properties."

Falov volleyed his gaze between the other three occupants. Everyone seemed to understand but him. He waited, expecting someone to explain, but nobody did.

"Just...drink slowly," Marius warned cheekily.

They toasted their glasses, and he noticed how the King and his consort were drinking something else. He opened his mouth to ask, but King Pasek quickly said, "We had enough fun in our youths already."

"You're both still young," Syrena chimed in as she sipped on her lubi drink.

King Pasek sighed, "I stopped drinking alcohol a few years ago because of my health. Marius followed along in solidarity."

Falov bit his tongue, curious about what exactly this drink was going to do to him, but let the meal commence. The faster they finished, then the more time Falov and Syrena had to search the castle for the Heart.

"Syrena, tell me more about how you two fell in love. I've heard his side, but I want yours," King Pasek smiled at her, and from her peripheral vision, she could see Marius' eyes lovingly on his husband.

The two of them had the best version of love Syrena knew. The seafolk were different from landwalkers. Royalty courted for alliances and regular mermaids found partners to spend their lives with, but even then, it often wasn't for love. With their species being hunted by the landwalkers, mermaids were constantly concerned with populating the sea to make up for the loss.

So whenever she saw their affection towards one another simply because of their deep love, Syrena craved to one day experience the same thing. At times, she resented the fact her kind didn't seek love out, and how one day, she would be stuck in a marriage for political reasons.

Then she met Falov.

Syrena cleared her throat. "I'm sure he told you how we met on the pier and how I snapped at him for drawing me."

King Pasek nodded. Everyone was listening intently. She couldn't let her eyes wander to Falov, even if she felt how he stared at her.

"After that it was a maelstrom. I accidentally tripped over a rope, fell into the sea, and shifted right in front of him. I didn't know how he would respond, but I definitely wasn't expecting him to jump in the water with me.

"At first, I thought he might be a mermaid, too, but that wasn't the case. He joined me because he wanted to."

"Might I add that there was a frosty chill coming from the Snow Court since they just completed their Undertaking. I was shivering in my wet clothes," Falov added as he sipped on his drink, the contents of the glass lowering to a concerning amount.

The King and his consort laughed.

"So he told me to come with him to his favorite tavern so we could warm up. We found a booth in the back corner and talked.

He flipped through his sketchbook and told me about his family, his friends, and his aspirations. It was so refreshing to see the world from his view as a landwalker. He had such dedication for the people in his life—and even for mermaids."

"That's an admirable quality," Marius sympathized as he dug his spoon into the citrusy mousse of the dessert on the table. "It's nice to hear of other landwalkers who have an appreciation for mermaids like us Balkovians."

King Pasek spoke up, "Agreed. Those pirates are violent creatures. All so they can participate in the Undertaking for some treasure."

Syrena refused to look at Falov, but she could tell he wanted to speak up. Pirates hated the Balkovians for abandoning the Rain Court, for refusing to be another helping hand during the Undertaking. Because as much as the Undertaking was a competition, it was also a fight for survival. Deep down, nobody cared what ship found the Heart, as long as one of them did. She directed the conversation away from this topic before tensions boomed.

"After that, any opportunity I had to get on land, I did. I couldn't get enough of him. Any minute apart felt like I was cut in half. Like I was missing *something*—because when we were together, I was whole again. It was strange and scary to have that dawning realization that a person can hold so much power. How did I live my whole life missing something I didn't even know existed?" The words slipped from her mouth, and she had no clue where they were coming from.

"Love is a powerful force," King Pasek chimed, stretching out his hand towards Marius, who grasped it tightly.

A pang of jealousy rocked her. Months ago, that was what she and Falov had, until it capsized into doom.

"It seizes you by the throat and holds you tight." It was Falov who spoke, and she closed her eyes, unable to withstand it but was forced to anyway. "I remember the exact moment, too."

"Tell us," Marius prodded without shame. Usually, she loved his breeziness. Today, she wanted him to shut up.

"One day we were walking the streets of my town, and all of a sudden there was a downpour. Most people stormed for shelter. I grabbed her hand, ready to lead her inside, too, but she pulled back, and quickly hid her necklace in her bag to keep it dry. I was confused, but she only stared up into the sky, letting the rain run down her face, and soak through her hair and her clothes. She said, 'let's dance.' There was no music, except for the patter of rain against roofs. I felt ridiculous, but I had no power to tell her no. I didn't *want* to tell her no."

"How romantic," Marius swooned.

Syrena's breath hitched, and she was unable to swallow her dessert. That moment with Falov had imprinted on her heart. Whenever she had clouds of sadness and grief canopy her, she thought back to how easy it had been then to dance in the rain with Falov—no matter how awful he was at it.

"As you can imagine, being a mermaid has hardened her, but I love that part of her. I love her bite. I admire it, even. But...It was her quiet joy that won me over, because it showed she was unafraid of the soft parts of herself."

"What was the moment for you?" King Pasek asked Syrena, innocently.

Syrena opened her mouth, but words wouldn't come out.

"She doesn't need to voice it," Falov said, then finished off his drink.

King Pasek and Marius shared a look, but she ignored it, relieved she didn't need to speak, because she couldn't answer the question.

"It's been a long day, I'm sure," King Pasek offered her an out, and Syrena thought that she could cry with relief. "I'm sure you want to give Falov a tour before you head to bed."

"That would be lovely."

"Your room is the same as you usually stay in," Marius said.

With that, their hosts stood from the table. King Pasek wrapped an arm around Marius' shoulders while Marius wrapped an arm around the King's waist. Syrena watched them go, wondering if she would ever allow herself to try to love again.

Eleven

As soon as Falov and Syrena were in the hallway, something felt off. Not about his surroundings or Syrena or their hosts. With *him*. His body tingled. Perhaps he should have heeded Syrena's warning and declined the second glass of whatever concoction he'd been drinking. Refusing to prove Syrena right, he rubbed at his eyes and shook it off.

Syrena noticed, though, because she rolled her eyes at him. Those damn brown eyes and her luscious, sweet scent that drifted over as she flipped her hair over her shoulder distracted him.

The whole dinner had been...strange. Even though it had been months since they had spoken before Syrena joined them on *The Dark Destiny*, he'd never stopped thinking about her. It made speaking about their time together easy and natural—hopefully enough to convince the royal couple of their marriage, especially when Syrena couldn't even form the words and lie about her affection.

They started walking together through the halls, which were lined with shelves filled with collections of treasure from under the sea.

Since the Balkovians sympathized with the mermaids, it made sense that the seafolk gifted them precious shells and pearls.

Speaking of pearls—Falov could not stop looking at Syrena. He was entranced by the sight of her. He always had been. That ethereal mermaid glow never left even when she shifted, but today, there was something extra magical about her. It wasn't just the clothes—or lack thereof. It was the fact she seemed comfortable and happy here. He hadn't been entitled to the sight for a long time, so he soaked it in.

"The Heart's not here, by the way. I don't sense it," Syrena announced simply, like so much didn't depend on this. He supposed Syrena and the seafolk—and even the Balkovians—lived in a blissful ignorance about the importance of the Undertaking, refusing to acknowledge that pirates murdered mermaids out of necessity and not desire. Or at least most pirates did. How did they not realize that they would all suffer the consequences if the Heart wasn't found each year?

He figured as much, but..."Are you lying in order to screw us over?"

Syrena stopped in her tracks. "Go searching by yourself then."

"I'd rather not." On Balkov Island, having Syrena by his side was a shield he regretfully required.

"Then you have to trust me."

He hated that even after all the betrayals, he did. He trusted her. No matter how fickle their relationship had become, Falov believed

Syrena didn't have the heart to actually hurt him or watch him get hurt.

The rest of the "tour" Syrena guided was mostly quiet. She provided a few details here and there, but mostly Falov remained quiet, looking on in awe. There were dozens of rooms with games for all the guests, two separate pools—because apparently the sea wasn't enough—and art the royals had collected over the decades. He didn't glance too long at those.

He asked about King Pasek and Marius.

Her eyes had softened as she told him their story. How the King was forced to marry, but he was being too picky, according to his parents. Then one day, Marius literally washed up on shore. He had swum beneath the dangerous sea to get through the hidden tunnels. King Pasek had been immediately smitten. Falov could tell Syrena looked fondly at their relationship, at the loyalty and love between them.

After looping around the castle, they were at their room for the night.

Syrena hesitated before pushing the door open. She didn't face him as she asked, "Why did you want to participate in the Undertaking?"

"Because I failed the crew last year and now my father is dead." His stepfather, too, but he didn't speak about that. It was tied to an event Syrena would need to be seated to hear about.

She blinked, seemingly shocked he was so blunt. "Wasn't it a storm that killed him? You can't control the weather."

A storm his father had refused to take seriously, and as a result, he and two other crew members had died.

"If I was there, I could have saved him."

She turned around. "Falov, you have a small drop of power. I don't think it would have been enough."

"I could have tried."

"Then you'd be dead, too." Syrena snapped, her eyes blasted wide.

Falov took a step forward, getting so close they were beginning to share breath. That earlier tingling sensation was now coming in full force, and his body wanted touch, it wanted skin and pleasure, but he stamped it down to have this conversation.

"Maybe Nyphadora would be alive then, and you'd be happy."

"I don't want you dead, either," she growled, though she hadn't disputed his claim either.

"Of course you do. That's why you lured that ship in our direction and enticed the mermaids to attack us."

"That's—" She stamped her eyes shut, as if trying to keep her composure. "That's just me trying to make your life difficult."

That honesty took him over the edge. He leaned over because his body was beginning to lose control. His nose was on her neck and he sniffed, notes of salt, and driftwood, and a hint of floral. His eyes rolled. He missed this so much. He missed her.

"Then what do you want?" His voice was low, his tongue tied as desire coursed through him.

When his gaze met hers, Syrena sucked in a breath.

"I don't know."

Grasping her waist, he started walking, leading them inside their private room.

"I want you," he admitted, then bit at her skin.

Syrena gasped, bending her neck back so her crown tumbled off, allowing him to take in more of her. As he continued down—aiming for what he wanted ever since he saw her dressed up like this—Syrena tugged at his hair, eliciting a moan from him.

His finger circled her right nipple, peaked and hard and ready for feasting. "I've been wanting these for so long."

"Is all this what you really want?" she asked breathily.

He stared at her breasts, ravenous for her.

"I'm not talking about me," she clarified.

His gaze snapped to her dilated eyes. The sight urged him on, but the conversation held him back.

"I don't think you want this," she said. "I think you've convinced yourself you do."

Falov didn't have words right now, his fingers still toying with her rosy nipple. Syrena was breathing hard, but there was no sign from her that she wanted to stop, so he went down on his knees and closed his mouth around her nipple, biting lightly.

The sound that escaped Syrena's lips jumped straight to his cock.

"Even when we did this often, I never had enough of you," Falov said as he focused on the other nipple, moving those gorgeous pearls so he could appreciate it fully.

And now, he wanted more. "Lay down," he ordered.

The command must have woken something in her because she pushed him away.

"Stop."

That one word was like a cold splash to his face. He got back on his feet and stepped away, giving her space.

"What's wrong?"

Syrena started rifling with the bed sheets, and turned away from him. "This isn't what you actually want. You're drugged."

"I'm what?"

She still didn't turn to face him. "The drink. The lubi flower. It has properties that make one...feral with desire."

Falov blinked, then swore under his breath. He was an idiot.

She was fidgeting with the pearl top, trying to unpin the clasp at the back, but her hands were shaking too much. He closed his eyes, ashamed of himself. She hated him. He knew this. Yet he still thought she would want to end up in bed with him.

"I'm sorry," he whispered.

She had no luck with the clasp, and she stopped trying at his apology. Her arms returned to her sides.

"It's not your fault. King Pasek and Marius like to play games."

"They warned me," he conceded as he took a deep breath, whatever effects of the flower had now completely dissipated. "Do you need help?" He gestured to her back where the clasp was still not undone.

She nodded, and he moved to her. His hands were quick, and he stepped away from her again.

"I can sleep on the floor," he volunteered.

"Don't do that."

"Do what?"

"Act like I wasn't enjoying myself."

"Then why are you angry?"

She whipped around. "Because by wanting you I am betraying Nyphadora."

And that was the crux of it all. Her resentment would always be a stain on whatever relationship they could attempt to have. A part of him was angry about it, another understood. The tangle of emotions would never loosen, it seemed.

"Just sleep in the bed with me. It's big enough for five people to comfortably fit," Syrena said as she put on a midnight blue slip the royals left out for her. Falov noticed his own set of night clothes in a pile by the window.

"I'll keep my hands to myself," he responded as the two of them got ready for sleep, neither further addressing what had transpired.

Unfortunately, his unconscious body had other plans. They woke up with Falov's arm around Syrena's waist and their legs inter-twined.

They peeled apart—exchanging no words. Each began to dress for their departure. Thankfully, Falov was provided with clothes that covered his whole body this time. The dark brown pants and linen shirt fit him perfectly.

Syrena, on the other hand, was given a simple, sage green dress. The cap sleeves and knee-length was modest in comparison to last night's ensemble, but the deep plunge at her chest still gave a taste of her generous cleavage. Half of her hair was pulled back, while the rest of the tresses were down.

"You look beautiful," he said, because he had nothing else to offer. It was true, though. She did. The dress reminded him of what she wore when she had visited him on land all those times. She liked blending in with the other landwalkers, she had told him. So much of life under the sea was about extravagance and treasure. Up above, she appreciated the simplicity.

A blush stained her cheeks, and he was proud he was still able to elicit such an innocent response from her. "Marius knows how to dress people for the occasion."

"We should probably go before it begins to rain."

They woke up to cloudy skies and humid air. There was a big storm coming, and he didn't want to be trapped on a small rowboat when it hit.

The halls were quiet, except for a few scattering of guards and servants. For the act—at least he told himself this was the only reason—he held Syrena's hand. She didn't object.

"The lovely couple finally awakens," Marius said with a mischievous smile. "I hope you had a fun night."

He winked at Syrena, and King Pasek bumped his shoulder against his husband's.

Falov cleared his throat awkwardly, "The bed was very comfortable."

"Where are you off to next?" King Pasek asked, changing the subject.

"Home," Syrena replied. "Nadmor."

"We need to find a ship willing to take us on," Falov explained.

"Be wary of pirate ships," Marius chimed in. "Those sneaky bastards are not to be trusted, especially with the Undertaking currently taking place."

Falov couldn't hold his tongue anymore. "I think those pirates are fulfilling their responsibilities. The Undertaking is essential to the survival of this court."

"Yet for some reason, the mermaids are the ones who suffer."

"It's the will of the Gods," Falov volleyed because, for some reason, there were too many people who struggled to grasp that it wasn't that simple. "We're all tools for the Gods' amusement."

"Who says that we must kill?" Marius asked.

"The ministers. Every year they have the same dream decreeing that the heart of a mermaid must be sacrificed to compete. If no one competes, then we'll all be dead."

"Those ministers are even worse than the pirates," Marius growled.

"I don't disagree," Falov acknowledged. "But their lives aren't easy, either. The resentment people hold against them puts them in danger."

"I heard that the last minister died unexpectedly," Marius said, but his voice held no sympathy for the life lost. "The Gods replaced him before his blood turned cold."

Falov nodded. "We're all cogs in a wheel, and the Gods don't like disruptions.

"You seem to know a lot about the Undertaking," King Pasek commented.

"We all should. Our lives depend on it."

"Questioning the Gods is foolish," Syrena jumped in. "We should go before they decide to rain down on us."

Falov looked at Syrena, grateful for her intervention.

Marius pouted but stretched out his arms to give Syrena a hug, saying his farewells, and lamenting about how Syrena needed to visit more often. Falov said his goodbyes to King Pasek, thanking him again for the warm welcome.

As King Pasek shook his hand tightly, he bent down to quietly say. "Be happy, pirate, I didn't have you killed. If you dare hurt Syrena, I won't be as gracious."

When they separated, King Pasek had an elegant smile on his face as he bid farewell to Syrena. Falov shook off the threat as Marius gave him a hug, too.

Within minutes, they were back in their rowboat with the open sea greeting them as they rowed back to *The Dark Destiny* emp-ty-handed.

※

Twelve

They swayed in the small rowboat next to *The Dark Destiny*. Falov had called up to the deck three times with no response. She could tell he was growing nervous. The whole crew had anticipated their return today, yet no one peeked over the rail to heave the rowboat up to the deck

"I don't like this," Falov muttered under his breath when he stood and the boat rocked. Syrena gripped the sides, as if that would help settle the craft.

"Careful," she muttered. "Maybe they're asleep, or trying to play a prank on us."

Falov shook his head, "They wouldn't. They take things seriously on the sea."

"Then we climb up."

Falov sat back down and rowed the boat over to the rope ladder. He extended his hand, and Syrena hesitated, the memory of last night flashing before her. Syrena could barely think about the incident without getting angry at her traitorous desires. Her body seemed to recognize Falov's touch on her skin, the rough calluses from years of working on a ship. Then, her mind would recall Nyphadora, and what those same hands had done, and she'd become nauseous at her own weakness.

She pushed past him and grabbed a rung, pulling herself up. She heard Falov mumble under his breath, but she ignored it, focusing on making her way up. With each step, she became more alert.

As her body leapt to the other side of the rail, she froze at the sight before her.

"Fuck," she whispered under her breath.

"Fuck," Falov repeated.

Across the deck, the entire crew were strewn, bound and gagged. Many of them were bloodied and bruised, as if they had put up a strong fight.

Syrena swallowed deeply when she caught a purple flag with a symbol of a mermaid tail tied on a mast.

"What happened?" Falov asked desperately as he unsheathed a dagger from his boot and began to cut through the ropes.

Syrena approached the crew, pulling down the gags so they could speak.

Lina was the first to respond as she rubbed at her raw wrist. "Bloody Balkovians."

"Where's my uncle?"

Falov's question was laced with worry, and Syrena couldn't blame him; the man was nowhere on the deck.

"In his quarters, I think," Mora responded. "They attacked us while he was down there, and we haven't seen him since. Either they killed him, or he's tied up alone."

Falov's face blanched, but he didn't allow his fear to take root—he kept helping his crew, ensuring each of them were out of the shackles. Syrena didn't stop either, and her heart clenched at seeing Luga's tear streaked face. She pulled down the gag, and he gave her a wobbly smile. Falov was by her side in an instant, cutting him free.

"So they just attacked?" Syrena finally asked.

Lina whipped her attention to her, the scales necklace flying with the motion. She had a note in her hands. "They were seeking answers."

"What answers?" Syrena hesitantly prodded.

"They thought we took a princess of the sea as a hostage."

Syrena snagged the note from Lina's hands. In it, King Pasek had written a warning to the pirates to release any mermaid they may be harboring against their will to his care. He had been weary as soon as the boat had sailed near to the island, because her parents had inquired about her. Apparently, they had been searching for her since she had been gone for so long without any correspondence.

"That's ridiculous," Falov muttered.

"We thought so, too," Lina spat. "Until the letter described someone with black hair and teal ends."

Mora stood next to Lina, her eyes inspecting Syrena. "No wonder Falov mentioned you were a tracker."

"I'm not—"

"Don't try to explain yourself."

Syrena eyed Falov, but he didn't seem to know what to do in this situation either.

Lina had stormed up to Syrena before she realized the woman had even moved. She stuck her fingers in Syrena's pocket and pulled out the shell necklace.

"Got you." She tilted her head to the right. "Though I had my suspicions since the moment Falov introduced you."

"We should find the Captain," Falov intervened.

"You go," Lina said. "She stays."

"No," Falov protested. "I'm not leaving her alone with you all."

"Then we throw her in the brig," Lina said.

Falov opened his mouth, but nothing came out.

"Let the Captain decide my fate," Syrena offered. "You are not in charge of this ship."

Lina swung the shell necklace right in front of Syrena's face then hung it around her own neck. Syrena gasped.

"Insurance that you won't just abandon this ship as soon as we let you go."

Syrena's shaky hands grasped at her bare neck. She was ready to plead to get it back, but Falov's strong hand was around her arm, tugging her away and down into the depths of the hull. Whatever outcome was about to be determined, she knew it wouldn't end in her favor.

Falov dragged his feet through the hall, his hand still around Syrena's arm. He couldn't let her go, fearful this would be the last time he would touch her in any capacity.

When they entered the captain's quarters, his uncle was tied to his chair, which was on its side on the ground. Seemingly, his uncle had tried to get out of the hold of the ropes.

Falov gritted his teeth as he cut through the thick layers of rope, and when his uncle was free, the man slowly got to his feet. Falov fixed the chair for him and offered his cane to him, but Captain Druz refused it. His uncle didn't look happy.

There was a note in a glass bottle on the table, and his uncle flung it on the cedarwood desk so it shattered. Syrena flinched, but Falov remained ramrod straight. Beads of sweat dampened the Captain's forehead.

"What does it say, Captain?" Falov asked, as his uncle read the letter that had been stuck inside.

"It says we should be very careful with the precious cargo on this ship. If they hear that Syrena was injured, the Balkovians will hunt us down until *The Dark Destiny* is at the bottom of the sea.

"I can explain—"

But Captain Druz put his hand up, stopping Falov from speaking.

"You are lucky we have not taken any help from that mermaid. If we had, we would forever be haunted by the curse of Skarb."

"It was always the plan to have her only push Mora in the right direction and never outright say where to go. I never would have endangered us like that," Falov countered.

"Yet you did," his uncle reprimanded. "Our crew could have been killed."

"The Balkovians are not bloodthirsty," Syrena reasoned, but it was the wrong thing to say.

"It's easy for someone of your kind to say that. They have no qualms with violence when it comes to us pirates."

"I'll make sure they never hurt you. I am friends with the royals there."

Falov was surprised by her defense of him, at her attempt to diffuse the situation. He expected her to delight in this lashing.

"*You,*" his uncle pointed the sharp end of the glass bottle at her, "have done enough."

"Put that down," Falov ordered. His uncle listened without pushback, taking the chair and sitting down. Falov could tell his old body had been drained by the ordeal.

"She is to be thrown in the brig for the remainder of this voyage."

"What?" Falov voiced.

"You are no longer my first mate. Lina will take over the role. You will be helping Luga as his subordinate instead."

"You wouldn't," Falov argued.

"I already did," was his uncle's only response.

Then the door opened behind them. Wysp was there, his one arm still in a sling, and his face dejected as he grabbed both of Syrena's hands, shackling her wrists together.

Falov shifted on his feet, ready to jump in, but Syrena shook her head. He didn't understand why she didn't put up a fight. Why wasn't she ripping out his uncle's throat for condemning her?

The last words Syrena heard before being ripped away from Falov were from the Captain: "This is for your own good, for the future of this ship. If you want to command it one day, you must take responsibility."

Thirteen

Falov was on his hands and knees, washing away the blood on the deck. As he watched the red strip away, he wanted to apologize to every crew member. He'd fucked up, *badly*. His father would have kicked Syrena off the ship as soon as she showed up. But Falov had let that piece of his heart that still hoped for her forgiveness to rule over his decisions. Now, he had failed the crew.

"You know we're not all angry with you," Mora said as she peered through her spyglass, hanging effortlessly on the shroud.

Falov snorted. "I doubt that. No one has spoken to me since we returned."

"Lina's orders. Also it's only been a few hours. Everyone's shaken up."

Falov sighed, standing up and wiping at the dirt on his pants. "Lina is pissed."

"Yes," Mora nodded, "but not for the reasons you think."

"Like what?"

Mora's yellow eyes scanned around them, as if checking they were alone before she leaned forward to whisper, "She's jealous."

Falov laughed, deeply laughed at the notion. "About what?"

Mora climbed down the shroud, getting on Falov's level. "Don't be an idiot. She gave up her chance at love to be a member on your dad's ship. She wasn't dumb enough to believe she would become captain when you were right there, but that doesn't mean she doesn't hold any resentment."

"I never asked to be captain," Falov muttered.

"You didn't turn it down either." Mora poked at his chest. "You could have told your dad no. You can still tell your uncle no. Yet, you stay."

Even though his mind had been in a lusty haze, he remembered Syrena's questions while they were in Balkov. Did he want this?

"It's not that simple. I can't just leave now. I'm the reason we even have a chance to participate."

"Lina would have taken the burden of getting a mermaid's heart."

"I have to do this for my father," Falov reasoned. "I failed him, Mora. I failed you all by not being on that voyage last year. I could have helped." His hands were clenched in tight fists, cloaked in swirls of water.

When he realized, he quickly let the water go, and it splattered onto the deck.

Mora smirked. "Your mother always wanted you to hide your powers because she wanted to keep her life in the sea behind her, but everyone on this crew knew the truth. You had no control of it as a kid, and we all at some point caught glimpses of it, but we kept the façade up to ease your mother's worries. Your father was proud of your abilities."

Falov examined the scars between his fingers, the ones he had looked at constantly whenever he sketched or painted. He had been grateful his parents had his webbing removed. It allowed him to have better mobility, it allowed him to explore what he loved. He hadn't picked up a pencil in months, though. "I never understood why the Weather Gods graced me with it."

"Perhaps they knew one day you would find a mermaid that would steal your heart."

"Syrena wants nothing to do with me."

"Maybe you need to prove to her that you will do anything to be with *her*, instead of trying to please us."

"So you're saying I should step away from this? The legacy my father set up for me?"

"If it no longer serves you." She shrugged. "Leaving this behind doesn't mean you'll no longer be in our lives. You're like a brother, Falov. Nothing will change that."

He looked up at the quarter deck where Lina and Captain Druz were chatting. Lina's gaze turned to him, a scowl on her face. Luga was with them, and the boy narrowed his eyes at Falov, pointing to the dirty deck.

"I should go back to cleaning before Luga gets upset."

Mora chuckled. "That boy loves the taste of power you've given him."

"He's committed to the cause. I can't blame him."

As soon as Luga heard he had a new helper, and that person was Falov, he'd rubbed his hands together in delight, as if someone brought him the biggest pile of treasure. Falov went along with the kid's demands. Luga deserved to feel in charge for a bit. His life had been so volatile, and this crew and ship were the one stable thing in his life. He felt at home here. Could Falov say the same?

"Think about what I said," Mora whispered into his ear, and he felt something drop into the pocket of his pants. He didn't reach for it, letting the moment pass over as Mora left.

He nodded before getting back to his knees and wiping more blood off the deck. With each stroke, he thought about what a life without *The Dark Destiny* and its crew might look like...could he live without them?

She heard rattling before she saw whoever intruded on her silence. Without a window, she had no clue how many days had passed since she had been thrown into the cell. She just knew her body began to ache, her skin becoming drier by the second. She needed to transform soon or else she would be stuck as a landwalker forever. Though, she had a feeling no one had enough mercy to allow her that reprieve. At least they had untied her when they'd locked her up.

"Even though I'm now in charge of Falov, I still can't order him to be the one to bring you your dinner."

Dinner. So it was nighttime.

"They wouldn't trust us together," Syrena easily explained to the kid who carried a plate with him. She noticed the balls of cotton in his ears. *Clever*, she thought.

"Lina said it's your fault we were attacked."

"Lina doesn't know how to keep her mouth shut," Syrena snapped.

"You don't always have to be so angry."

"I'm not angry," she said through gritted teeth, then loosened her jaw.

"Falov mentioned you don't eat meat, so I brought you cheese and bread."

Syrena's head bowed lower at the mention of Falov's name. She didn't know what to make of everything that had happened between them. She was still angry and hurt at what he had done, but he continued to show concern for her and fought for her well-being. She didn't know if that would ever be enough for her to move past the grief.

"How is Falov?" she asked, though, unable to help herself.

"He mopes around the ship."

She wasn't surprised. That man wore all his emotions on his sleeve. She loved that about him.

"Where are we heading?"

Luga zipped his mouth shut with his fingers. "I was given orders not to say."

"Of course not." Syrena sighed, and leaned back, looking up towards the ceiling where swirls of colors were painted on the ceiling. She had noticed it immediately when she was placed inside, and she knew the culprit of the drawings.

"What's that?" Luga reached his small finger through the cell doors, but he couldn't get very far. "On your neck."

Syrena touched where he pointed, but she couldn't crane her neck in a position to see.

"It looks like a bruise. Did the Balkovians hurt you, too?"

Syrena scrunched her brows, because they certainly hadn't—then it hit her. Falov's mouth sucking on her neck, feasting across her skin like he was a man starved. Her face heated.

When Syrena didn't respond, Luga said, "You're not very good company. You barely talk."

"There's not much to say when you've spent days stuck in a cell."

"It's only been a day."

"Has it?" Damn, it felt like weeks. Maybe she was being dramatic. If it had only been a day, she still had time to convince someone to let her in the water to shift.

The boy didn't leave yet, his eyes on her legs.

"Ask away, Luga."

Luga's eyes widened, as if he didn't expect to be caught staring. But he sat down in front of the cell, crossed his legs, and removed the cotton from his ears, like he expected to stay awhile. "Are you really a mermaid?" his question was hesitant, almost scared.

"Yes," she answered simply. She wouldn't punish him for being curious.

"Do you like the sea?"

"It's my home. I love it." Though sometimes it no longer felt like home without Nyphadora.

He patted his chin, thinking. "Does your skin prune like mine after I swim too long in the sea?"

"No." She laughed. "Not even when I'm in my human form."

"Do you have a pet dolphin?"

Syrena hadn't anticipated the conversation to head in that direction. "No, we don't keep any of the animals as pets. They are their own free spirits."

Luga took in the information, nodding along as she spoke.

"How about you?" she asked, wondering if the boy ever talked about his own life, if he was ever given the chance to.

He shook his head. "I've made friends with some rats before."

Syrena instinctually stood up, wiping her backside, and inspecting the cell for droppings. Luga chuckled, the sound so light and carefree. The boy was *young*.

"Not here, silly. On the streets of Nadmor."

"Why were you on the streets?" Even as she posed the question, she already knew what his reply would be. "I had nowhere else to go. Not until Falov found me and gave me a home here."

Syrena swallowed the lump in her throat. She couldn't understand how this sweet man— the man she had grown so comfortable with—had done what he had to Nyphadora.

"I should go before someone notices me gone for too long. Or you sing me to sleep."

"I would never," she promised.

He narrowed his eyes, but then shrugged it off.

"Wait!" Syrena called.

The boy turned around, his face expectant.

"Thank you for the food and for the work you do on this ship. Even if no one else says it, you're appreciated by the crew."

Luga stared at her for a moment before he said, "Lina told me not to let flattery sway me to help you."

Syrena was left with her mouth agape as the boy bounded up the stairs.

Fourteen

Syrena woke up to the rough sway of *The Dark Destiny* and the sound of the wind howling. Her stomach lurched as the hull dipped and rose, her body straining as she held onto the rusty gates of the cell door.

Oof! She wheezed as a metal dinner plate slid and hit her arm.

Luga had turned off the oil lamp for safety reasons, and without a window, she was cloaked in complete darkness. She guessed a storm raged outside. Skarb had been gentle with them so far, so it seemed it was time for him to test the pirates.

The wood groaned from the pressure of the water. She instinctively grabbed at her neck, only to find it still bare. She swore under her breath. If she couldn't shift, she wouldn't be able to breathe underwater.

Yelling sounded from somewhere above. She was on the bottom level of the ship, sleeping with all the extra supplies—somewhere easily forgotten if something went wrong. She doubted anyone would think of her if the ship went down.

She roughly tugged on the cell door, but it didn't budge. She was trapped. *The storm would pass,* she tried to convince herself. It was just another obstacle in the long game. Soon the sun would shine, and they would be back on their way to searching for the Heart. Though, without her skills, the crew may never find it.

Right as she took a deep calming breath, she felt something tickling her bare feet.

Water.

Falov had barely slept the past four days. He felt stripped down, and not because his title had been taken from him. He barely cared about that. It was the knowledge that he was at fault for Syrena's jailing. Why had he offered her a position on this crew? He should have shoved her away when he had a chance, should've protected her from this outcome.

But he knew why: he'd selfishly wanted an opportunity to explain himself. It was stupid. The longer he thought about what he'd done—how his hands would be forever tainted with Nyphadora's phantom blood—he knew he'd never be able to forgive himself. So how could he expect Syrena to?

That moment had been so quick. He'd barely had a chance to think through his actions. One second Nyphadora had a blade at his stepfather's throat, the next Falov had his own blade in Nyphadora's abdomen.

Now, he stared at the sand slowly funnel down from one side of the hourglass to the other. They were about halfway through the Undertaking, and they were nowhere close to discovering where the Heart was. But he watched Nyphadora's heart become more covered by the sand with each second. He itched to grab it, to run down into the hull of the ship and give it to Syrena—along with her shell necklace. He owed her that.

Before he could contemplate it too much, he stumbled forward, using the table in front of him to break his fall.

He heard Lina yelling orders, and he knew the moment of reflection had passed. They had a storm upon them, and his crew needed his hands.

He ran up the stairs to the deck of the ship and was met with bedlam. The crew was running back and forth, trying to decipher their orders, but the whipping winds made it hard to hear. Falov's clothes were immediately soaked as the rain pelted at him.

He trekked against the wind to get to the quarter deck, where Captain Druz had just commanded to strike the royal mast. Crew members jumped to action.

Falov overheard Lina and the Captain discussing abandoning course and sailing with the wind. This storm was serious. If they made one wrong move, the ship could end up in the bottom of the sea, exactly like the Balkovians wanted. At least his uncle was taking the storm seriously, unlike his father had.

Falov squinted against the rain, looking to the horizon, but it was pitch black. It was too dangerous to try and sail anywhere safely. Swearing to himself, he trudged up to his uncle.

"What do we do?" he screamed against the roaring weather.

His uncle's face was serious as he held onto the wheel of the ship like it was his cane, his grip tight as he maneuvered *The Dark Destiny* through the massive waves. He could tell Captain Druz was becoming weak, and that only heightened Falov's guilt. Instead of accepting his destined role as captain, Falov decided to spend the year as a grieving bum.

"We pray Skarb has mercy on us," Captain Druz responded.

Falov glanced at the crew, every hand that helped to ensure they made it out alive. He wondered what it was like last year during that fateful storm. Did any of the crew hold guilt about his father's death? Did they think they could have done more?

"Get off this ship, Falov," his uncle said, causing Falov to blink in confusion. "I know those powers will get you out alive. Keep swimming west, and you'll reach land."

"I'm not leaving you," Falov argued. "I'm not abandoning them—or you."

The boat tipped to the side, and Falov slid until he hit the railing, his body almost pitching overboard. He groaned as he centered himself back onto his boots.

His uncle's countenance turned more serious. Falov could see how he was grinding his teeth, his jaw tense. He was holding on to that wheel like it was a life source. His uncle should be in his quarters. He should be letting Lina steer, but such a suggestion would only anger him, and Falov needed the captain calm.

"I'm not going to be responsible for your death. Your mother wouldn't be able to handle it after losing so much already."

"But—"

"You do not owe anyone on this ship, Falov."

Falov shook his head, retorts swirling in his mind. Even in the chaos, his uncle's voice was steady.

"I see it in your eyes each day. Your father looked the same every time he left your mother to get on this ship. That guilt won't serve you, like it didn't serve him. Go! Before I push you off."

Falov wanted to fight. If *The Dark Destiny* went down, he would go down with it, with the rest of the crew.

"Take her and go." His uncle stressed each syllable.

Panic engulfed him, his hand immediately digging into his pocket, where Mora had dropped the shell. Syrena would die if she couldn't shift. The pressing reality had him stumbling across the deck and scrambling down into the lowest depths of the hull. As he left the last stair, he stepped down with a splash There water licking at his ankles.

Fuck.

From where he'd left the door ajar, faint oil lamp light trickled in, reflecting off the water and their prisoner's skin. Syrena was holding onto the grate of the door, her chest rising and falling as she breathed heavily. She was scared.

"Syrena," he heaved out.

She looked at him, those brown eyes wide with a silver sheen. He pressed his hand over her fingers.

"We're getting out," he reassured her.

He snatched the key from the opposite side of the room and unlocked the cell. She jumped onto it, and they both fell back into the puddle. She was on top of him, her hands at his throat.

"Where is it?"

"I have your necklace," he assured.

"Not that. Her heart."

Falov blinked, his mind unable to catch up with what she wanted, but then he realized she meant Nyphadora's heart.

"We can grab it when we go."

Her hold on him loosened, and a tear finally escaped, the small bead dripping down her pretty face.

"I need to find wherever the water is coming from first, and we can go."

Syrena pointed directly at the hole. It was in the back corner behind crates of supplies. The sudden movements of the ship must have caused the sharp corners of the wooden boxes to splinter the wall.

Syrena climbed off him, and he stood. Falov quickly gathered old pieces of wood and rusted nails that were lying around, and hammered them until the leak was sealed. It would have to do for now.

Syrena stayed, observing him as he moved.

When he finished, he offered his hand, and she took it.

Before he'd left to help on the deck, he had hidden Nyphadora's heart in the crew's quarters. There were cots lining both sides of the wall, and a few hammocks hanging from the ceiling.

He heard sniffles, and then he saw Luga curled up on one of the cots. Syrena stiffened beside him.

"Kid, what's wrong?" Falov bent down so he was at Luga's level.

"I'm going to die."

Falov sucked in a breath. "You're not going to die."

"Captain Desh died in a storm."

The words clogged something in his chest. His father's fate was still a sore spot to more than just his own heart. "My father died because he acted irrationally"

Syrena was now on her knees in front of the boy, too. "Nothing bad will happen to you. Come with us, and we will protect you."

Luga shook his head frantically, wiping at his nose. "I can't leave *The Dark Destiny*."

Falov stepped in. "There is no dishonor in protecting yourself when it calls for it."

"I won't go," the boy's voice shook. "This is my home."

Falov looked at Syrena, but her eyes were on Luga.

"If something happens to you, I promise you will be protected by the mermaids below. They will keep you safe."

Luga was quiet, unsure of how to respond. Even Falov had not been expecting such a declaration.

"I'm not supposed to trust mermaids."

Syrena smirked. "We are a bloodthirsty kind, but we would never hurt a child. They'll even introduce you to a pod of dolphins if you ask nicely."

Luga hesitated but he nodded, accepting the offer.

Falov took the chance to go to the last cot, and opened a small trap door beneath it. He pulled out the hourglass, and Syrena gasped, her hands instantly reaching out. Instead of handing it to her, he stuffed it, along with a few other supplies, in a canvas bag.

"We need to go," Falov urged, lugging the canvas bag onto his shoulder. He gave one last look at Luga. "Stay safe, kid. You'll do great things for this ship one day."

Then Syrena and Falov were off, running to the gundeck.

"Are you leaving?" Mora's voice called from behind them.

They both froze, as if they'd been caught. Even if Captain Druz had given Falov permission to release Syrena and abandon ship, he still felt like he was doing something criminal.

Mora's yellow eyes and hair were like a beacon in the darkness of the ship.

"I—" Falov started, ready to explain, but Mora shook her head. "Good."

"Is this goodbye?" His words were soft, hesitant.

"No." Mora shook her head again. "More like an 'I'll see you around.'"

Falov nodded, liking the sound of that. At least right now with all the chaos surrounding them. Tomorrow would surely bring regret.

"Stay safe," Mora said.

Syrena turned away and started to run, but Falov held her hand and pulled her back.

"Wait!" he shouted. Syrena stopped as he put down the bag, and pulled out the necklace from his pocket. Syrena dipped her head so he could secure it around her neck. Then he swung the bag over his shoulder, and together they dove out the gunport of *The Dark Destiny.*

Fifteen

Pebbles bit into Falov's skin as he crawled up the shore, his breaths labored and his eyes burning from the saltwater. His bubble had lasted about halfway through their swim towards land before he needed to resurface. With each stroke, his regret for leaving the crew grew.

He heard the crunch of the pebbles behind him. They were smooth beneath his hands and knees. Syrena came to stand next to him, looking out at the land they'd washed ashore on.

"I have clothes in this bag," he hitched a breath, pointing behind him to the old sack on his back.

Even though she was backlit, he could see her roll her eyes at him. The sun hadn't fully come out, but it was behind the clouds, causing them to glow.

"You keep forgetting I have no problem being naked."

Falov sighed as he pushed himself off the beach, his eyes following Syrena's.

"We have no clue where we are and who else is with us. You're too vulnerable like this," he reasoned with her.

"Good thing I know exactly where we are." She gave him a devilish smile.

Falov swore under his breath as Syrena started marching inland. The colorful pebbles—translucent orbs with swirls of blue, green, and purple inside—bit into his bare feet, but he kept up with her seamless pace. It looked as if someone had taken paintbrushes and dipped them in different colors, pressing dots all across a canvas until it was a cacophony of colors. Trees hid what lay beyond, but as they trekked deeper, the pebbled beach turned into stone paths.

Syrena was also barefoot, though she didn't wince once.

"Would you like to explain where we're going?" Falov muttered as he avoided the cracks in the stones. He didn't need to embarrass himself by tripping over.

She didn't deign to answer his question. Her hair was soaked, the dark and teal clinging to her wet body. He had to force himself not to look at her.

He huffed, mumbling under his breath as they crossed a small stream. "I saved your life and you still can't stand me."

Syrena stopped, and he had to anchor his toes in the ground to not bump into her. Although the rain had stopped, the leaves from the trees dripped water on them, and he blinked when one hit his eye.

"It's not that simple." Her voice was low and shaky. "Saving one life doesn't make up for taking another."

He wanted to shake her and force her to turn around. "What happened that day isn't that simple either, Syrena."

"Don't you dare." The words were cold, her anger stimming deep.

"You avoided me for months. I could barely face myself, the guilt of what happened, and then you disappear. I wasn't angry. I understood it even. But then you show up on *The Dark Destiny* ready to steal Nyphadora's heart, and instead of sneaking around, you're in my room easily caught." She was still turned around, but he trudged forward. "I think you wanted me to catch you, as if your body desired the truth. Yet, you can't allow yourself to give into that desire."

Her shoulders tensed slightly, but she finally faced him. "I don't want to hear it because I'm scared."

It felt like his body was being consumed, sucked in by quicksand. Those words hit something deep, the truth puncturing.

"I'm scared that learning what transpired that day will make my feelings for you revert back to what they once were. I'd be betraying Nyphadora—because no matter the explanation, she's dead because of you."

Falov could have sworn he heard Nyphadora's heart beating from within his bag, but it was just his own pulse thrumming in his ears.

"I can't control how you will feel afterward, but I do think you owe it to yourself to hear it."

Her eyes closed. "I don't want to taint my memory of her."

"She's not the villain. No one in this scenario was." Even if everyday he fought the bile rising in his throat as he remembered his hands covered in Nyphadora's blood.

"If I listen, will you give me her heart?"

He almost laughed at her negotiation skills, but he had no fight left.

"There was never a scenario where you didn't get it back," he responded without hesitation.

She stared at him, her eyes reserved. "Let's keep walking for a bit," she said.

He nodded, but he took her hand in his, and she didn't pull away.

They were quiet as Syrena led them forward, but the sound of crashing water intensified as they moved through the thicket of trees. She tried not to think about the conversation the two of them were about to have—one long overdue—but every time she snuck a glance at the man walking beside her, her heart rate increased.

A part of her wanted to take Nyphadora's heart and leap back into the sea, never to see Falov again. But he was right, she owed it to herself to hear the story, even if the pain it would cause frightened her. All she had left was the glimmer of hope that the other side of this story would stitch together the frayed part of her. She had a feeling Falov would be waiting with the thread and needle.

"Woah," Falov gasped as they stepped out from the copse of trees.

Before them poured a waterfall, the rush of water created a peaceful atmosphere. The lake that pooled beneath was as clear as glass, and as they approached they could see fish weaving amongst the rocks. The same array of colorful pebbles as the shore lined the bottom of the lake, and a rainbow glimmered on its surface as a result.

"How did you know about this place?"

Memories flashed before Syrena's eyes of Nyphadora and her playing in the water, jumping off the cliff on top of the falls as landfolk and landing in the water as mermaids. They collected the glossy pebbles as tokens. They could hide here, and the rest of the world didn't matter.

A light squeeze of her hand brought her back to the present, where Nyphadora would now always be a memory, easily lost in the wind.

"Maybe we should sit down," Falov said as he guided her over to the lake's edge.

Syrena wiped at her burning eyes, and sat down with him along the shore. Falov dipped his feet in the water.

"It's warm," he said.

Syrena nodded as she dove into the lake, her body transforming in an instant. When she resurfaced, she pushed her wet hair back from her face. "The fish here are magical. They have heating properties. There's not enough of them to make the water hot, but just enough to make it tepid."

Falov hummed as his eyes scanned his surroundings. She saw his right hand twitch as if he thought he had a pencil in his hand. She wanted to ask him when the last time he drew was, but she held back.

He blew out a breath and tied his damp hair back. "Everything that happened that day, happened in the span of minutes. I did not wake up that day anticipating to kill. I didn't even think I had the ability to take a life, but the adrenaline in that moment proved how anyone has that power, especially when protecting the ones we love."

Syrena's heart stuttered, tail swaying beneath her body, but even the comfort of the water was not enough to staunch the wound that was being ripped open. She had foolishly hoped that she would be wrong, that Falov had not been the one to land the killing blow, that he was hiding the true identity of Nyphadora's murderer. But the truth slipping from his mouth brought back that brimming rage that she had held onto.

"My mother and father separated ten years ago. I was only twelve at the time, and I was heartbroken, especially when less than a year later she was marrying the minister of the Rain Court. A man who I hated because, as a kid, I blamed him for being the reason my father left each year to participate in the Undertaking. As I grew older, I realized that wasn't a fair assessment. The man had to follow the will of the Gods, and the Undertaking needed to be completed in order for our court to survive another year.

Yet after they separated, I noticed a slight shift in my father's mood. He had become depressed because he needed to kill a mermaid each year to participate, yet lost every time. I think my mother tried to get him to stop, but the only ones brave enough to compete in the Undertaking were the pirates, and he felt duty-bound."

"Pirates have such egos," Syrena muttered under her breath.

Falov snorted. "When my parents split, life wasn't much different, honestly. I lived with my mother at the minister's manor, but I worked with my father on *The Dark Destiny*. Outside the Undertaking, the ship takes various voyages across the continent, pilfering merchant vessels with goods from other courts. Yet, when it came time to the Undertaking, my father refused to let me join the crew. He said it was too dangerous. I fought him on it for years, but he kept reminding me that he needed me alive to take over the crew if something happened to him."

Falov swallowed. "That day, I was walking back home after helping the crew repair something on the ship. As soon as I got close to the minister's mansion, the energy shifted. Something was off. I rushed inside and was greeted by the sight of Nyphadora with a blade to my stepfather's throat. My mother was in hysterics, a knife in her hand. She was ready to kill Nyphadora if something happened to her second husband. I was thinking through what would happen to Nyphadora, even if my mother hesitated. If the town learned, it would be seen as an act of treason. She would be issued a death sentence, and the execution would not be peaceful.

"Nyphadora saw me, and she moved the blade closer to my stepfather's throat. My mother yelled and stepped forward like she was about to charge, and without thinking twice, I took the blade from my boot and threw it. It struck Nyphadora in the abdomen. Her last words were addressed to you: *Don't let this stop Syrena from living and loving.*"

Syrena's body shook in the water, the warmth not enough to soothe her. What he'd just told her was insane. Nyphadora would never hurt anyone.

"My actions weren't enough to save my stepfather. I didn't even realize the blade was already in the man's throat. The minister of the Rain Court had died, and I just became eligible to compete in the Undertaking."

"Why was she there?" Syrena's voice was raspy.

"I have no idea. To avenge justice on behalf of all mermaids, perhaps?"

Syrena thought back to all those times Nyphadora and her were together when in Falov's town. She had a guilty conscience when she abandoned her friend to spend time with Falov, but Nyphadora never seemed to mind. Nyphadora would always wander off for hours, entertaining herself. There would even be times when Syrena waited on the pier for her, so they could head back down to the sea together.

"It doesn't excuse what I did, and I understand if the truth isn't enough to forgive me, but I'm not a cold-blooded murderer."

"But you will have to be."

"What do you mean?"

"I mean that you're about to become the captain of *The Dark Destiny*. You'll be required to kill a mermaid each year to participate."

He shook his head. "My father was obsessed with the idea of finding the Heart and winning at least once. So much so he let that unhealthy desire consume him. I don't feel the same way."

"Yet, you haven't declined it. The whole crew thinks you're taking the role next year."

"I'm—" He hesitated. "I'm not sure what I'm doing after this. I'm learning more and more that I don't find it worth it. The expectation of leading is creating tension on the crew because they know my heart isn't in it, and the whole fucking thing is the reason I lost you."

Those last words came out in anger, a frustrated rush as he roughly rubbed at his eyes.

"Would you have competed this year if you hadn't killed Nyphadora?"

"No," he responded quickly. "I would have found a way to be with you."

Syrena was so lost. The rational part of her warred with the one that craved the past, where it was Falov and her—the one where Nyphadora was still alive.

"And what are you going to do now?"

He extended his hand to hers. She didn't hesitate to give him her webbed hand, and allowed him to place it over his chest, so she could feel the frantic beat of his heart. "I would rip out my own heart for your forgiveness."

Syrena's breath hitched at the revelation. He looked so defeated with his head bowed. He had been torturing himself for so long, holding it all in. He wasn't proud of what he'd done, and Syrena still had so many questions about Nyphadora's presence in the minister's house that day. But she didn't let those ruminations hold her back. She pushed herself up, using Falov's legs to anchor her, so that half of her body was out of the water.

"What if I wanted to be the one to rip your heart out?"

Falov lifted his head, those blue eyes glittering. Their lips were so close—just one movement and they would be touching.

He didn't seem scared of her half-hearted threat. "I would let you do anything as long as I could call you mine again."

It was so much to take in all at once. If she was acting rationally, she would step away from this, allow herself time to think. But she had been ruminating on them for months, refusing to entertain even the thought of the two of them this close together again unless it was when she had his pulsing, bloody heart in her hand. Yet...she couldn't help the way he made her feel so safe and seen, even when he was admitting to a crime that had ruined her.

She pressed her lips to his, barely a featherlight touch. "That's a big promise to deliver on."

"I am yours to command," he said against her lips, still waiting, still hesitant. He was allowing her to make the call.

She thought through everything he had said, the emotions he'd displayed. Even in the past few weeks while she worked against him, he had always been on her side. He'd defended her against the people she knew he called a second family. He allowed her to make her own choices. He'd saved her from that cell.

Nyphadora was gone, and she wasn't coming back. She could either let the pain fester and hold her back, or she could let it flow into something new.

She inhaled, threw off her necklace, then deepened the kiss.

Sixteen

Her body tingled as it shifted into its human form, and the throbbing between her legs was insatiable. She had missed the way Falov wound her so tight before he tore her apart again in a blissful release.

His hands were all over her, and she fumbled with the ties of his pants. She was ready to rip the fabric apart to get what she had craved for months.

"Careful, Princess. I'm not going anywhere." His voice was low, and she hated how calm he was. She was starving with need, frantic with pulsing desire.

"Take your clothes off," she growled, and a huff of laughter escaped his lips as he nibbled on her neck.

He pulled away, and even in the warm water, an icy chill swept over her at the loss of his presence. He stood up, and she craned her head back to watch as he took off his shirt, revealing the lean muscles beneath. Then he undid the knot on his pants and pulled them down to reveal his erection. She almost pushed herself out of the water, but he leapt in with her. She turned around right as he broke the surface.

He was on her before she could blink. She gasped as her back hit the edge of the lake, her body contorting to fit perfectly against his. Falov's hands were on her cheeks as he devoured her, their tongues tangling together for dominance. She had her hand pressed against his chest, and his heart vibrated against her palm.

She moaned as his mouth left hers, his lips traveling down until he was at her breasts, feasting at one hardened nipple, while pinching the other. Her head dropped back, delighting in the overwhelming sensation. The cloudy sky above began to pour down on them. The rain was cold against her face, but Falov's heat kept her from shivering.

She was so lost in his ministrations that she didn't have a second to prepare before his finger found her clit.

"*Oh.*" Her body trembled as he explored her folds.

His mouth was still on her breast, and he looked up at her. "You like that," he purred around her nipple, as his finger dipped into her core.

She shut her eyes tightly, unable to use her voice as a second digit entered her. She was grinding against his hand, forcing him to go faster and harder. He satiated her by quickening his pace, two fingers inside while his thumb flicked at her clit, until she had no idea what was up or down anymore. She just knew that she was on the brink of orgasm, and nothing outside this little oasis mattered.

She pulled his face back up, kissing him again, needing his breath to keep her afloat as she shattered around his fingers. The sensation was so intense she saw stars. She was floating in her own bubble of euphoria. He bit her bottom lip as he helped her down from the heights of her pleasure.

Their chests were both heaving, creating ripples and small waves as they lay against one another in the lake.

"That was so—" he started.

"Get inside me," she commanded before he could finish. It wasn't enough; she didn't know if it would ever be enough. She had denied herself of him for months, savoring the anger that had grown because of what he'd done. Yet, he'd known the truth, and he'd waited until she was ready to know it too. Now, she couldn't resist him any longer.

"I'm not going anywhere," he repeated, but this time the words were met with a whisper of a tear sliding down her face.

She wrapped her legs around him.

"Put me inside you," he said.

She didn't hesitate. She found his length under the water, aligned it with her entrance, and guided him home. Both of them breathed deeply, Falov's face falling into the crook of her neck as he perfectly fitted himself inside her. Neither of them moved at first, simply enjoying the warmth of each other's bodies. There would be other times for fucking until they walked away sore. Today, she wanted to feel all of it, to memorize what he did to her and what she did to him.

She grasped his shoulders, which were slippery from the rain, and his arms were on both sides of her, caging her against the edge of the lake. He slid out and thrust back in slowly, setting a sensual pace so that she could relish every inch of him.

"I dreamed of this day," he whispered against her skin, each word punctuated with a thrust. She moved her hands to his scalp, threading his long, soaked hair between her fingers. Each push inside her had her craving more. He moaned, and she wanted to be able to replay that exact sound forever. Perhaps one day the Lightning Court would invent something that would allow her to do just that.

They were so close to each other, and each time he was seated fully inside her, there was friction against her clit, and it jolted another shot of pleasure over her whole body. She whimpered as she craned her left leg close to her chest, allowing him to angle himself in a way where he could hit her deep, innermost wall.

"Keep going," she whined into his ear, biting the lobe.

"I never want to stop."

Each thrust made a moan escape her lips, growing louder as her second orgasm skimmed the surface.

"I missed this," he said. "I missed you." He kissed her deeply, and her eyes fell closed, allowing him to lead her over the edge.

But it were his next words that had her core tensing and her body spasming as a blissful release echoed out of her.

"You're my home," he chanted like a prayer.

It only took two more pushes before she felt the warmth of his release inside her. His breathing was uneven, and she kissed his neck and shoulders, easing him out.

It was too much. It was not enough. She wanted him forever, she wanted never to be parted again. She realized then that he was her home, too. Even in her anger, her inner soul had guided her to her true north star.

"We should do that again," she teased to lighten the moment. He only growled as he pulled her away from the edge of the lake until they were swimming together in open water. Syrena laughed openly and freely, and she had missed that sound, the relief of it. She hoped Nyphadora heard it from wherever she was now, and knew her closest friend was beginning to repair the wound her death had wrought.

Falov couldn't believe the past few hours had been real. He pinched himself so many times, he was starting to form a bruise on his arm. Syrena smirked when she noticed it, but then she would kiss him and remind him that this was in fact real.

The words he said had been true. All his life he had been seeking a place to call his home. The small house when his parents were married, the minister's house after his mother remarried, *The Dark*

Destiny. Yet, finally he recognized his home would never be a place. It was a mermaid.

Syrena wore her necklace again, diving into the lake to explore the water below. Falov joined her, his bubble allowing him to take it all in. The lake wasn't as deep as the sea, but even then, it was a different world beneath the surface. The fish nibbled on his toes, and he found unique plants below. Syrena ripped a few of them, but she didn't explain why.

They were now sitting behind the waterfall to hide from the rain; the entrance of a cave loomed darkly behind them. They were naked, Syrena's head was in his lap. Even so, there was nothing sexual about it. The weight of her on him was the most familiar, comforting feeling.

He leaned back on his hands. "Is the Heart in there?"

Her face didn't move, and her voice remained neutral, giving nothing away as she responded. "I can't tell you that."

"You didn't worry about stating your opinions before."

"I never interfered with where you chose to look," she responded sternly.

"So even then you were looking out for me, for the crew."

Syrena was inspecting her nails, refusing to look at him. He wouldn't have that. He tugged on her chin, forcing her eyes in his direction.

"You cared even when you hated me."

She shrugged, clearly desperate to make the notion seem like nothing when it meant everything to him.

Then, he thought about the crew he left. The people he called family. He wondered where they were now, praying they all were safe and that *The Dark Destiny* suffered no major damages.

"Thank you. For protecting the crew, even when they weren't on your side," Falov said.

"I think I swung Luga to my side in the end."

"And Lina..." he started, trying to find a way to explain to her. "Lina seems to have a complex history with the seafolk. I think we were a reminder of what she gave up."

"It's not our fault she regrets her decision."

"It's not that," he clarified. "I think she resented that she gave up love and still wasn't rewarded with what she wanted most. With what she deserved."

"Which was?"

"To be captain."

"And will you have any regrets if you move forward with becoming captain like it was destined?"

The question hung in the air around them. He let the sound of the waterfall soothe him as he thought about his answer, but Syrena spoke up first.

"You're forcing an answer. I see it in your eyes. For your whole life, you've been trying to fit into a mold that has been created for you."

"I already failed my father once." His voice cracked. "I failed you and Nyphadora. I don't want to fail the crew by abandoning that role."

"You failed no one."

"I did." He couldn't stop the tear that formed, the wave of regret breaking down the dam he tried holding together for so long.

Syrena was biting her tongue, and he could tell she wanted to ask more, to comfort him, but she didn't. As if she recognized she couldn't be the one to convince him.

"We should go," she announced, the sound loud enough to cause an echo in the cave. "Get you back home. I also need to head home for a while and explain where I've been, what I'm doing next."

Falov nodded. "What *are* you doing next?"

"I think a large part of that question depends on you," she said, and her voice was a little sad. It hurt him to hear it. Falov brushed his fingers through his hair, thinking about his future and what he wanted it to look like. It was a blurry frame, but somewhere in the center of it he saw wisps of teal and black and an iridescent glow.

Seventeen

Falov searched the cave just in case the Heart was inside. He came back empty-handed, exempting the new bruises he would be sporting on his legs after bumping into too many stalagmites.

A part of him wanted to drown under all the pressure, while the other part was still determined to find the blasted Heart so he could offer it to the crew as an apology.

He created an inch of space between his thumb and index finger. "I'm only a little annoyed that I had to do that when you already knew it wasn't there."

Syrena was clothed again, as was he, but when he left her, she was skimming rocks against the lake. Now she was holding the hourglass. Her hands gripped it tightly.

"What happens to all the mermaid hearts after the Undertaking?" she asked.

He knew she was asking because he'd gotten an intimate look into the life of a minister. He'd witnessed how his stepfather would spend hours praying atop the cliff at the minister's home. "The minister burns those from the losing crews and keeps the one from the winning crew."

"So they're trophies for his pleasure?"

"I don't claim to understand the purpose of it." He came up behind her, gently placing his hand on her shoulder, looking down at the organ inside the sand. Because of the storm and their harrowing escape, the hourglass no longer told them how much time remained before the Undertaking ended. He only hoped *The Dark Destiny* and its crew were alive and still searching.

"Nyphadora deserves a proper burial," Falov commented. "You should take it with you."

Syrena shook her head. "I can't. Not if you still have a chance of winning this."

"I don't even know where we are," he rubbed his temple, exhaustion hitting him. "We need to find a rowboat or something to get us back on the continent."

"Falov," she turned around, throwing her arms around his neck, the hourglass still in her grasp. He responded by wrapping his arms around her waist. "We're on the continent."

Falov had been staring at her eyes, lost in their depths, but when her words registered, his head snapped up. "We are?"

"Yes." She chuckled.

That sound was enough for him to forget everything that still had to be done. He dipped his mouth to hers, swallowing her laugh so it consumed him inside and out.

"And you want to come back with me?"

She nodded. "For a bit."

Although they were on the Rain's Court's soil, it took them almost the whole day to leave the wilderness and venture back to society. The rain had slowed to a drizzle.

It was strange to be back. He realized then that Nadmor had always been just a place to him. It had never held his heart. He could live anywhere, and as long as Syrena was beside him, nothing was missing.

He felt more hopeful now in comparison to when he'd left on his voyage for the Undertaking, but he was still just as scared. It was like he had been walking a tightrope his whole life. When he'd left, what was in front of him was darkness and the unknown. Now, he saw the glimmer of light at the end, but he was still on the rope, his body swaying as it tried to balance and not fall. He didn't want to lose what he'd gained.

The streets were busy, but no one glanced twice at them. They had no clue who he was, or that he had a mermaid at his side. They walked the path towards the boarding house. After everything that had happened, he had to find lodgings away from the minister's house where his mother still lived. As guilty as he was for leaving his mother to not only grieve her first husband but her second as well, he knew he wouldn't be any source of comfort for her.

"I always loved these roads," Syrena commented beside him, washing away his thoughts so he could focus on her.

Instead of grout or dirt between the stones, there were veins of water; big enough for fish to weave between the rocks, traveling from the sea, through Nadmor and back.

"It's fascinating how the fish know the way."

Falov scrunched his brows. "It's not like they're going anywhere specific."

"Are they not?" Syrena tapped her chin. "They seem to be getting around with ease. Look over there," Syrena pointed to the bakery. "The fish flock there at the end of the day, when the baker comes out with stale bread."

Right on the mark, the baker stepped out, crumbling the unsold bread into the water.

"I guess,." Falov shrugged off the notion that the fish were a clever animal. They just wandered aimlessly. "We're here."

They entered the old building. The smell of herbs and roasted meat assaulted his senses, and his stomach growled. It had been so long since they'd eaten, especially something delectable and filling.

He was already dragging Syrena up the stairs, though. Food could wait.

The stairs creaked below them, and they dodged a few other patrons before reaching his room. Rifling through his bag, he found his key and unlocked the door.

"I'm surprised that it didn't get lost in the sea," Syrena commented.

"Skarb had a little luck to spare, I guess," Falov said as he opened the door for her. She let go of his hand as her eyes gazed around. He crossed to the chest at the foot of his bed and opened it, pulling out a map of the Weather Continent. He unrolled it out on the bed.

"This is where it's been hiding." Syrena's voice was light, curious.

"What?" He turned to her. She was looking through his chest, taking out his sketchbooks, digging deeper to find his charcoals and paint sets. Then his paint brushes were in her hands, her fingers trailing against the bristles. The handles were pearlescent—the brush set had been a gift from her. She had them specially made for him, but shortly after he'd received them, everything with Nyphadora, his mother and stepfather happened. He had thrown away a lot of his art and supplies because he couldn't stand the sight of them. However, whatever was in this chest he hadn't had the heart to part with.

"Why do you hide them?" she asked.

"Because they serve no purpose."

She blinked, her lips slightly pouting, and he wanted to nibble at her mouth so she would smile again.

"But you love art and drawing and painting. When we were together, you always had your sketchbook nearby."

"A lot has happened since then."

"Do you miss it?"

He sucked in a breath, contemplating the question. Did he? There were times when he was on *The Dark Destiny* and all he wanted to do was pick up a pencil and sketch his surroundings, or to draw Syrena from memory. It had taken great restraint not to allow himself to transfer life to paper.

"Yes," he replied simply. "I miss what drawing allowed me to relive and refeel. Whenever you left me, I would draw you, and I could live in those special bubbles of moments we shared again. It made days without you less difficult. Or there were times I drew my father on *The Dark Destiny*, with his captain hat on, his spyglass in hand, and I was able to be that small kid again who always looked at him with awe."

"So you deny yourself now. Why?"

Falov exhaled deeply as she pushed again. He didn't know what she wanted from him. "I—"

"Is it because it's not beneficial for being a captain?"

"Partly," he grumbled.

"But you don't want to be captain." She gestured to the multiple sketchbooks that surrounded her. "You want to draw."

It was almost laughable how easily she could admit a truth Falov was still grappling with. He grew up expecting his life to steer in one direction, but as he aged, he began to consider what other lives he could live. When Syrena and he met and began to fall for each other—because that was exactly what had happened during those months together—he'd added a future with her in with the possibilities. Yet...

"That's not enough," he pressed.

"It could be, if you wanted to. You act as if the weight of *The Dark Destiny* is on your shoulders, like you have to follow your father's legacy. From the sounds of it, you have more than one path now."

"It's not that simple."

"It *is*," she pushed, but when he said nothing else, she grunted. "When King Pasek and Marius questioned what moment it was when I began to fall for you, I couldn't answer it then. As we trekked here, I finally discovered an answer. It's when I learned you sat at the pier for hours everyday waiting for a mermaid to come up on shore so you could hand them one of your drawings. I was too busy to visit you for a few weeks because we were hosting guests at our castle, yet you did everything you could to make sure I had a reminder of you. I received ten drawings in three days. Each one made me smile more than the last one. Nyphadora teased me, saying how she had never seen me smile so much. I felt *seen* and *special* and..." She swallowed. "Loved. And now I need to show my love by reminding you that you have to finally make the choice *you* want. Stop listening to the crew, your uncle, and even me. Decide for yourself. You were gifted powers that no other landwalker has because your mother stepped away from the sea to be with your father. She made a choice. Now, it's time to ask yourself, what is your future, Falov?"

"I can't answer that right now." He glanced back at the map, his hands shaking because he was losing grasp of the situation. "I have to try to find the Heart."

She stood up, and Falov began to feel like the rope was swaying beneath him. He was seconds from falling. "Then, I'll wait for you until you do. But I can't stay and help you."

There was a double meaning there; she couldn't help him with finding the Heart, but she also couldn't be the one to guide him to the path of his future. It was on him to do it.

"I'll be back after the Undertaking." Syrena headed for the door.

"Wait!" Falov shouted too loudly. "Your plants."

He knew she liked collecting things and bringing them below. He went into his bag, pulling out the different plants she had excavated from the lake.

"Those are for you," she announced. "If you dry them out, their petals and stems make great colorful powders you can mix with water, to paint with."

Falov barely had a chance to take it in before the door snicked shut. Syrena believed in him in a way he couldn't fully grasp. Now, he was alone with Nyphadora's heart, a map, Syrena's gifts, and all his art supplies to taunt him.

Syrena didn't stop once on her way to the sea. She wanted to get off land and back to familiar territory. The last day had garnered a monumental shift inside her. She no longer felt the incessant rage she had once held onto, but she ached with emptiness, an utter sadness at knowing when she finally returned to the sea, Nyphadora wouldn't be there.

Her mind bounced with reasons as to why Nyphadora had been at the minister's mansion that day, why she had planned to kill the minister. The hatred between the seafolk and landwalkers was mutual. Yet, no one would be dumb enough to kill the minister of the Rain Court. As Falov had said, it would be a death sentence, one more torturous and brutal than the one Falov handed her.

She jumped off the pier and into the sea, her iridescent tail flipping smoothly as she traveled back home. The deeper she swam, the darker it got. But as she kept going, the ocean began to brighten again. There were schools of various varieties of fish sweeping past her, other mermaids passing by, sunken ships that had been pilfered of treasure. It was a whole society under the sea, and even though they were a different species as the landwalkers, they still had hearts that beat. Syrena was proof that those hearts could also learn to love.

Basalt structures littered the seafloor, many of them simple homes, others built with spires to declare them homes for royals—though being a royal was barely unique. She had seven siblings ahead of her. It was why she felt no pressure about becoming queen one day. She lived her life like she had no responsibility whatsoever, which might have been why she didn't understand why Falov felt the pressure to become captain. To her, there were many options if he truly wanted to step away. It was that damn guilt stopping him. He had to realize he couldn't blame himself for every wrong thing that happened in his life.

"There you are!" a familiar voice screeched jovially as she came around a large boulder.

"Marisha!" Syrena smiled at her second oldest sister.

"You've been gone so long, Mother and Father actually noticed you were missing. They even sent a letter to the Balkovians." Her sister snorted.

It was a recurring joke between her siblings. With there being so many of them, it was not uncommon that their parents lost track of all their whereabouts. Syrena actually liked it. It allowed her not to worry about alarming her parents when she decided to randomly leave. Though when she left to get Nyphadora's heart, she had not expected to be gone as long as she had. Perhaps learning that their grief-stricken daughter had left with no word was worrisome enough to start asking around for her.

"I got tangled up in something," Syrena said.

Marisha linked their elbows. "Well, everyone wants to see you." She began tugging Syrena forward, but Syrena pulled back.

"I actually have to do something first."

Marisha narrowed her brows, but her face softened. She must have seen something on Syrena's face, and Syrena didn't like being read so easily.

"I'll see you soon," Marisha's voice was smooth as she left.

Syrena nodded as she told her sister, "let Mother and Father know I'm safe."

She couldn't get distracted with her family right now. They would badger her with questions. She needed to get her own answers first and that required visiting somewhere she hadn't been since Nyphadora's death.

Eighteen

Syrena pushed aside the stalks of seaweed jutting from the seafloor like tendrils of thick hair, and shoved aside a large rock that covered a small entrance into an underwater cave. The hole was small enough she had to shimmy her way inside, but when she got through it, the space widened. When Nyphadora and Syrena were younger, it was a lot easier entering and exiting, but as they grew, it had become a nuisance. Syrena constantly pestered Nyphadora that they should find a new spot, but her friend refused.

So all their trinkets stayed.

The whole cave was covered in chests they had taken from pirate ships over the years, and all of them were filled to the brim with jewelry, utensils, cups, compasses and more. Some of them couldn't even shut because of the overspill. They had no purpose for any of these things, but there was something special about the secrecy of the place, about the adventures they had taken to acquire the goods. It was theirs, something they'd built together.

Now, it was just hers, Syrena supposed. She no longer shared it with her closest friend. These objects were meaningless without

Nyphadora. It was the stories that had accumulated together that would fill the cavernous hole in Syrena's heart—the one specifically for her friend.

She opened the chest to her right, and she was overwhelmed with the amount of stuff inside. She sighed as she picked up a pearl necklace, and then looked around the room. This would take a while.

Two days later and Falov still didn't have the Heart. He'd searched various shops, dug under trees, and hiked hidden trails that led him further inland. He had begun to wonder if the Heart was at the bottom of the sea.

It wasn't impossible for the Heart to be hidden amongst the sea flowers. There had been a few years where the pirates had found it below, and had risked their lives to obtain it. It was rare though, and a dangerous dive to obtain it.

Falov was becoming defeated. He felt like he owed it to his father to find the damned thing so at least, postmortem, his father could say *The Dark Destiny* finally was a winner, and that his obsession over the years hadn't been in vain.

Falov sat at the pier, where seagulls dove down at him on too many occasions, trying to steal a bit of his garlic bread. He wouldn't allow it.

He inspected the map of the court again, desperately seeking anywhere else he could explore. His eyes kept wandering to the home on the west side of town, on top of a cliff overlooking the sea, where a building was marked with an eye. The minister's house. His mother still lived there, since the new minister was gracious enough to let her stay as long as she needed after his stepfather's unexpected death. It was a big enough home that she and the new minister likely rarely crossed paths.

He'd been circling around the premises ever since he'd started his search, but he always found excuses to avoid it. He wondered if his mother knew he was back on land, or if she was blindly living her life worrying about his whereabouts. *I should see her,* he told himself. To assuage any of her worries. But...that building held so much baggage, and he didn't know if he had the strength to face it.

A seagull pecked at his leg, and he swatted the bird away. Another came down at him, and another, until he was being attacked. He threw the blasted bread into the sea, and a swarm of birds followed.

Falov wiped his pants, grabbed his map, and headed off. He couldn't delay this any longer.

The minister's home was in an isolated part of town. As the path inclined up, the roads that were previously woven with water were now cleanly paved. His legs began to burn as he reached the top of the hill upon which the building sat.

The iron wrought gate squeaked, and his attempt at remaining calm failed. The door to the house opened, and an older man exited. He knew that to be the valet, and he didn't even question Falov, just allowed him inside. The foyer was expansive, and across from it massive bay windows overlooked the cliff and the sea beyond.

"She's in the back garden," the valet announced as he inspected Falov's shoes. He couldn't blame the man. There were too many occasions where he'd trailed in dirt and water onto the pristine sage and cream tiles after returning from *The Dark Destiny.*

Falov saluted the man, then went to find the woman he had been avoiding for too long.

His mother looked peaceful, surrounded by the greenery. There was a small pond at the center of the gardens and the whole space was surrounded by bushes, creating a private haven. Bees buzzed around and birds chirped nearby.

"Hello," he said quietly, as not to startle her, but she barely moved as he sat next to her on the wooden bench. Her hands were occupied by a locket necklace made from a clam shell. He knew that inside was the silver-banded pearl ring his father had proposed with.

"You're back." She sounded tired, but also relieved. "There's still time left, so either it went very well or very badly."

"The latter," he confessed. "Well, not *very* badly."

"Your father would always do the same. He'd downplay the enormity of the Undertaking, pretend everything wasn't as bad as it was even if he came back with broken limbs or black eyes. Whenever I tried to warn him to stop going, to stop obsessing over it, he wouldn't listen."

"So you left him."

She was opening and closing the clam shell in her hand, exposing and hiding the ring inside. "I mitigated his depression."

Falov stilled. "What do you mean?"

At first, his mother remained quiet. He gave her a once over. The long sweep of her brown hair had been pulled up in a knot on her head and her simple cotton dress was perfectly pressed. Even if she had lost her tail permanently, he could tell the mermaid lived beneath her still. She had a fluidity in each of her movements. Her body, even as it reached fifty, had not succumbed to pain or hardship. She moved around the world easily, and he hoped one day she would finally decide to step outside the walls of this mansion to see it.

Her blue eyes—the same shade as his—looked into the pond. "Your father wanted to win more than anything. He fought endlessly to do it, but he—like many other pirates—*hated* having to kill the seafolk to participate. Every year when he took that life, I could tell how it ripped something vital within him. He felt like a monster for killing, and then losing each time."

"It's the way of the Gods. Skarb tells the minister the requirements, and we must listen."

"So we thought."

He shook his head, having trouble processing those three simple words. "I don't understand."

"The order of the ministers is corrupt. They feel powerful because of their Sight and their connection to the Gods—even if they have none of the power of their respective courts. And we all blindly follow them."

"Are you saying they're lying?"

She snapped the necklace shut. "I'm saying they can do whatever they please, and we don't question them—so I left your father to marry one. Your stepfather promised he would allow your father to compete without having to kill, if I did. Since I remarried, he was eligible to compete without getting any more blood on his hands."

Falov took in all the information, not able to believe any of the words leaving his mother's mouth. There was no way that pirates had been killing the seafolk for decades—centuries maybe—all because the ministers wanted to prove their power.

"Why are you only telling me this now?"

"Your father and I didn't want you involved. It would make you liable, and we couldn't risk you."

"Stepfather agreed to this?"

His mother shrugged. "A marriage was breaking up because of it, perhaps it was enough for him to agree. Though, I met him before I met your father, and we had one night together before I left back to the sea. The next time I came on land, I bumped into your father and our connection was electric."

"I just—I can't believe it. All this death for nothing. The long feud between seafolk and landwalkers is fabricated because of lies."

"We're stuck, Falov. In order for the courts to survive, we must listen and follow orders."

"The seafolk deserve to know."

"If they learned the truth, they would be killed," his mother said easily, the truth slipping from her tongue like she'd once had the same thoughts coursing through her.

"How can we live with this truth and not do something about it?" he asked.

"Because the other outcome is more death. Perhaps one day, someone will be brave enough to fight back against the ministers and the Gods to save this continent. Today, we can only live to survive."

Falov thought about Syrena down below in the sea, the anger she'd had about her kind being killed. If she ever learned the mermaid's deaths were not required, he knew she would rage until the sea parted and Skarb, himself, had to intervene.

"I don't know if that's good enough for me," he replied.

The benefit of being a mermaid was that as long as she was in the sea, a source of food was always close by. She didn't need to venture far to gather seaweed, so she stayed in the hiding hole for days—slept there, too. She wouldn't leave until she'd found what she needed, even if her hands cramped and her muscles ached. She'd do it for Nyphadora.

Ten chests were sorted, but she still had about another ten to go. Nothing provided her any clarity about *why* Nyphadora had been on land, determined to kill the minister.

Over the grueling hours, slips of paper with Falov's drawings had distracted her. She'd gotten caught up, thinking about their past. The times where they laid in bed together, both satisfied, and he would pick up his sketchbook and draw something for each time she'd left him. Many occasions they were images of her. When she asked him why, he replied he wanted her to know how he saw the world and her from his eyes. It was in response to when she once proclaimed how she wished she had an artist's soul, so she could see the wonder of her surroundings in a different light. He had remembered her desire and promised to deliver on her wishes in the only way he could.

Syrena sat on a ledge, her tail swaying. She rubbed at her eyes, wishing something would appear before her. What if there was nothing here? What if Nyphadora had just woken up bloodthirsty one day and decided the minister was her target? There could be so many possibilities, and none of them might offer the closure she needed.

She huffed deeply, shoving the chest until it fell over the edge. It hit rocks on its way down, and everything tumbled out. Sighing, she looked at the mess and felt the sting of tears. She wanted Nyphadora back, she wanted Falov to choose a life with her in it. She didn't want to fight alone anymore.

She swam down to start putting the things back, but when she looked inside the empty chest, she noticed a crack in the wood. She pressed on it and it gave away easily. Punching through, she found there was a hidden layer, and in it were sheets of paper. Letters addressed to her, in Nyphadora's handwriting.

Syrena's heart stuttered as she glimpsed those pages. Then, she devoured them, unable to restrain her desire to have her friend back even for a little longer.

Each letter devastated her more. Under the sunshine smile, Nyphadora had been in so much pain and anger. She had found love with a pirate with an undercut, and gray eyes like a storm, and that love had been ripped away from her. She wrote of their friendship, how much it meant to her, but how she couldn't live with the fact seafolk were dying at the hands of pirates. She wrote about how happy she was that Syrena had found Falov, but that she was frightened it would lead to the same heartbreak she had experienced.

Then, she wrote about searching for answers. How she believed there had to be another way, and then how she'd stumbled into a tavern one day, where she overheard a man drunkenly slip out how he was the minister. She'd followed him home, broken in, and learned a truth that had her stomach rolling inside itself. When Syrena read what Nyphadora discovered, Syrena's body went numb. She barely recalled herself hiding the letters in the chest, and swimming up to the surface, ready to rip apart anyone who'd had a hand in the lies.

Nineteen

Falov had his sketchbook next to him and a pencil in his hand, twirling it between his fingers. His eyes focused on the sea as his mind juggled all that he had learned of the morbid truth his mother had just revealed. Corrupted ministers didn't surprise him, but he'd never suspected they would go so far as to be the root of so much bloodshed.

Now, he was condemned with the truth, unable to decide if he should keep silent or tell everyone. The seafolk deserved to live, to not be hunted each year. But the consequences would be dire.

There were only two days left until the Undertaking ended, and Falov had not found the Heart. He attempted to convince himself *The Dark Destiny* had found it, that they would come back as winners and give his late father what he always dreamed.

But he didn't see the ship's black flag on the horizon. He picked up the sketchbook and opened it. Pages and pages were filled with his old drawings, and he saw the progressions of his skill. As a child, he was glued to his sketchbooks, and his father had to pry them out of his hands whenever they were on the ship so he could focus on his chores. Now, he couldn't remember the last time he'd put charcoal to paper.

So he fixed that.

With shaky hands, he allowed himself to wander the page, to let his heart guide him to create whatever called to him. It was messy and unrestrained, but his hands moved with ease. Even if it had been almost a year, it was like coming home. The familiarity of it was transcendent, and he sat there for hours drawing until the pages were covered with new art. Midday turned to dusk, and the sun dipped behind the horizon.

As he got up and stretched, his body cracked. But Falov was pleased with himself. Maybe even proud for allowing himself to get lost in something that had once meant everything to him.

He readied to go back to the boarding house, his body a little lighter now, even with the weight of a damning truth pushing down on him. He was smiling to himself, which earned him a few strange looks from passersby. He didn't care. He only wished Syrena were with him; she would have been proud, too. Her absence caused a new ache in his chest. He missed her. Is this what life would be like if he decided to captain *The Dark Destiny*? He didn't like it. When he thought of his future, she stood at the center of it—his muse for whatever eternity the Gods would grant them.

An errant glimmer caught his eye. Falov looked down. He blinked. And the only conclusion he could come to when he saw a fish with iridescent scales was that he needed sleep. He must have been hallucinating, so desperate for Syrena's presence that his mind was playing tricks.

But even after rubbing his eyes, the fish remained, swimming through the cracks in the streets. Syrena's words bubbled up to him: fish always knew where to go.

Without hesitation, he followed.

This was not normal behavior. He considered abandoning this strange mission of following the iridescent fish, but every time he considered stopping the pursuit, the fish doubled back as if encouraging him on. The sky had transformed from a blend of oranges, purples, and pinks into dark shades of blue. The humid air told him rain would start pouring soon, but his eyes never lost sight of the fish.

With only two days left until the end of the Undertaking, he had nothing to lose anymore.

They were still in the main part of Nadmor, the late hour meant people were heading home for the night or were heading to the tavern for a drink.

"Where are you going?" Falov whispered as he followed the fish around a corner, passing dark-windowed shops.

Of course, the fish didn't respond—only continued its journey with a flip of its fins. The sparkle of its scales were so reminiscent of Syrena's that Falov almost drowned in his own misery. It was a different pain than when they had last been apart. When Nyphadora died, there was a bottle of mixed emotions between them that needed to be cracked in order for them to heal again. Then, circumstances outside any of their controls that had kept them apart, even if Syrena hadn't known that at the time. Now, her absence was solely on him. All he had to do was give up the title he had dreaded inheriting to build a life with her. It was so simple. Yet, he held back.

Falov blinked when he walked right up to an old building at the furthest point of a dead end road. The fish was swimming back and forth beneath the shop's entrance.

Falov tilted his head to the right to read the embossed sign.

Rain Court Antiquities

Although the shops behind him seemed to be closed for the night, he could see through the window that the lights were still on in this place. He stepped inside, a light jingle sounding from above him.

Immediately, he was overwhelmed with the display: shelves stacked to the ceiling and filled to the brim with every manner of object under the sun; old furniture, trinkets, and so many lighting fixtures above him he had to squint for a second to adjust to their shine. It was an assault on the eyes, and on top of that, there was a mildewy, dusty scent that made him want to sneeze. As a pirate, he could easily call it a treasure trove of sorts—not one a pirate would fawn or fight over, but there would be something in here for anyone to appreciate.

"Welcome," a gentle voice called out from somewhere deeper in the shop. Falov couldn't see them, but he heard footsteps inch closer.

"Hello," he responded when a woman close to his age stepped around a shelf. Her brown hair was braided and her brown dress was covered in dust.

"Is there something I can help you find?"

He opened his mouth to speak, but nothing came out. He couldn't just ask this woman for the Heart.

He found the first excuse that slipped from his tongue. "I'm looking for a gift."

Her eyes lit up. "What's the occasion?"

"An apology gift. But also an 'I want to spend the rest of my life with you' gift."

She nodded, taking in his words so carefully she didn't blink. "I'll begin looking around. Feel free to scour. There's always the unexpected in a place like this."

Falov did as she bade him, leaning closely to look at the small statuettes or to read the titles on the spines of books. There was a whole section dedicated to pocket watches. Most seemed to be broken, but they were beautifully made.

The back corner caught his attention. Every inch was dedicated to art. Paintings, sculptures, drawings—every medium one could think of was represented here. He flipped through the standing stacks of frames, seeing what artists had created. There were a mix of landscapes from across the continent, portraits, and abstract works with no solid shape. Each piece was uniquely made by the hands of someone compelled to bring their vision to paper. He got closer to the back of the third stack when his hands stopped.

It was a painting of this exact shop and in the bottom corner he saw his own signature. Or, he should say, the scribbles he'd made as a child to represent his signature. He pulled the painting out and cringed. His strokes were off, the colors poorly blended.

"My mother found that painting along with a couple other ones a few months ago, abandoned in the streets. She was sad to see such beautiful work left alone like that. I think that's the only one that remains. The rest have been bought," the shopkeeper said.

Falov thought back to after he'd thrown that blade at Nyphadora, how his fingers had gone numb with regret. When his hands wouldn't cooperate as he attempted to sketch after her murder, he had abandoned some of his pieces, unable to stomach the sight of them.

He hadn't remembered ever painting this, though. He had been a child, so it was long ago, but this shop didn't exist even in the darkest pits of his memory.

"My mother mentioned how one of the captains of a ship...I'm trying to remember its name." She tapped her chin and her eyes widened as she remembered. "*The Dark Destiny.* Apparently, its captain would come back each year after the Undertaking to donate some of the treasure they had discovered during the competition. I guess once, a young boy had been with him, and my mother noticed him on the ground, drawing the outside of her shop."

Falov still had no recollection of that. But what was more surprising was how his father had brought treasure here. Was it his version of penance, an attempt to remove the dark stain on his heart?

"Anyways." She waved off the story. "My mother homed the drawings and paintings here, and they sold well. Perhaps, I should hang this one up."

"I feel like the artist would like that." His voice was scratchy. Emotions flooded the forefront of his mind as he thought back to that young version of himself who soaked in the world around him. Young Falov hadn't restrained himself from what his heart desired.

"Does this beloved of yours like jewelry?"

Falov nodded at the woman, and she guided him to the back of the store where there was a glass counter displaying jewelry. Gold and silver, pearls and gemstones.

But there was a velvet box in the corner—teal, the same shade as the ends of Syrena's hair—that caught his attention.

"What's inside that one?"

The woman smiled and opened the box for him, where a heart-shaped emerald gemstone glistened against all the lights above.

Syrena pulled her body onto the pier, her tail turning into legs. She grabbed the pack she had always kept hidden in a barrel for her rendezvous with Falov and changed into a set of clothes. Her body trembled with anger, but as soon as she was clothed, she stormed into Nadmor, her sights set on one location.

She must have appeared disheveled because all eyes turned in her direction. She ignored them, even though all she wanted to do was scream. Mermaids had been taken advantage of for decades. Even if these townspeople didn't know the truth, they were all culpable in her eyes. Too many of the seafolk were dead for nothing. Her best friend was dead because she had learned the Rain Court's dark secret and had dared to confront the minister.

Syrena's hands tightened to fists as she reached the large home on the cliff and swung the gate open.

Twenty

Falov found himself at the pier again, anxiously awaiting *The Dark Destiny*'s return. Other competing pirate ships had arrived back, and the pirates' defeated faces clued him in on their disappointment.

Every few seconds he tapped his pocket, ensuring the Heart was still there. Since he had found it, he hadn't parted from it. Every time he passed by anyone, he had a strange, gnawing feeling they knew the Heart was in his possession—that they would pounce and steal it from him for the sake of winning both treasure and glory. He hadn't gone to the minister yet, but time was running out. There was only a day left, and if he didn't present the Heart to the minister soon, the Rain Court would be in trouble.

Yet, he still waited for the crew to return.

It was only midday, but the skies were gray. Last night's storm had let up, but another was brewing, and it would only strengthen if the Heart was not returned in time.

When the worries grew intense, he tried putting pencil to paper. Falov *wanted* to draw something, but he was so unstable, it was impossible to even make a straight line.

He couldn't believe he'd had artwork that sold. Artwork that wasn't even that impressive. Never in his dreams could he have imagined anyone would care for his art enough to use real coins to buy it. That revelation had struck something deep within him. It made that once foggy future become clear. No longer was he balancing on the rope, unsure of what was in front of him. He could see the life he wanted to build for himself, and the people he wanted by his side.

But even as he faced that pretty picture, he knew getting there wouldn't be easy. There were still tough choices he had to make and people he needed to talk to.

And as he paced the wooden pier, the gray clouds looming above, he almost cried in relief at the sight of familiar black sails on the horizon.

Syrena shoved the man that opened the door for her and stormed into the grand entrance of the house, slipping on the sparkling sage and cream tiled floors as she did.

"Miss, where are you going?" the voice behind her nervously called, but she didn't answer.

She had one goal in mind—and it was ending the life of this fucking minister and every mininter that followed. She could understand exactly how Nyphadora had ended up in this home with a blade to that man's throat. The anger that pulsed through Syrena was debilitating, and it could only be washed away by bloodshed.

The house was quiet, but she deciphered sounds of life from somewhere above. She ascended the winding staircase two steps at a time, not giving herself a moment to hesitate.

Laughter sounded from a room at the end of the hall, and when she burst in, a man was lying in bed with a woman next to him. Their nudes bodies veiled under the thin sheets clued her in to exactly what the two had just been doing. Luckily, mermaids didn't care about propriety. She approached the man whose eyes were wild with fear.

"You piece of shit," she seethed.

The woman fell out of the other side of the bed, and fled from the room without any clothes on. *Good*, Syrena didn't need an audience for what she planned to do to him.

"Your kind are evil," she hissed.

"I don't—what do you—" the minister stammered.

"You think tricking pirates into killing mermaids for sport is funny?"

The man shook his head so fast and hard, Syrena thought his head would pop off his neck.

"Adding your dead body to my collection sounds so pleasing," Syrena said as she pulled out a blade and pressed the tip to his exposed chest.

"Please," he begged.

But Syrena had no mercy to give.

The Dark Destiny docked, and Falov waited for the crew to come ashore. If this was the past—when Falov watched as his father came home with his crew after another Undertaking—he would have jumped aboard the ship, excited to see everyone again.

Slowly, one-by-one, the crew disembarked. Each passing face looked more tired and defeated than the last. One of them was immediately hounded by two women who began yelling. That must have been the one Lina had tattled on. Luga ran down the gangplank and immediately caught sight of Falov. The boy waved.

"Falov! Falov!" he shouted, turning everyone's attention to him. Falov tried hard not to cringe.

Falov ruffled Luga's hair. "You've completed your first voyage."

Luga's smile somehow grew even more at Falov's proclamation. "And I didn't even die once!"

Falov laughed, pride swelling in this chest. Luga's enthusiasm would get him far. Falov pulled a coin from his pocket and leaned down to whisper. "Go celebrate, and buy yourself something fresh to eat."

Luga didn't even pause for a second before he swiped the coin and ran off.

"Glad to see you in one piece," Lina said as she approached him while Mora helped his uncle down the gangplank to ensure he didn't fall.

"I can say the same to you. Looks like *The Dark Destiny* kept you all afloat."

"Only sustained small damages that should be easy to repair," Captain Druz said, leaning on his cane.

"Thankfully our next voyage won't be for months," Mora said as she rested against a wooden pillar where she moored *The Dark Destiny*. They all looked so exhausted.

"I abandoned you all," Falov said quietly, struggling to look any of them in the eyes, but knowing he had to.

"Because I told you to," Captain Druz emphasized.

Falov shook his head. "Someone dedicated to the ship, someone who is lined up to step up as captain, would have stayed regardless of that order."

"I couldn't risk you getting killed. Your mother would never recover."

"Still..." Falov took a deep breath. "It's not fair for me to claim the title, especially when my heart isn't in it."

"What are you saying?" Mora asked.

Falov looked directly at Lina now. "I'm saying there is someone better equipped for the job."

Lina's jaw clenched. "I don't want it out of pity."

Falov rolled his eyes. He was handing her what she wanted, and now she decided to be noble about it. "You've earned it."

"I didn't earn shit."

"Look in my bag," Falov gestured towards the brown satchel that rested on the dock.

Lina scrunched her brows but bent down and opened the satchel. He knew it wouldn't take her long to find it, though there was a long stretch of silence where she didn't move. Her body was frozen—likely in shock.

She turned around, and her hands emanated a green glow.

His voice was soft as he said, "Good job, Lina. You found the Heart."

Silence followed. He could feel Mora straighten, his uncle stiffen.

"What the fuck, Falov?" Lina hissed.

"See? You brought honor to *The Dark Destiny*. I think that calls for a new title, right Captain Druz?"

Saying his name shook his uncle out of his confused daze. "I think that sounds exactly right."

He was grateful his uncle could move on, too. He had devoted his life to his brother's mission to win an Undertaking. It was time for Druz to rest.

"What comes next for you?" Mora asked as she went to Lina and poked at the emerald gem, as if testing if it was real.

"It's not all figured out yet," he announced transparently. "But I know the bits and pieces of it and that's enough to allow me to sail forward."

Lina approached him, her face and hands tinted green from the glow radiating from the Heart. "Thank you." She swallowed. He knew showing emotion was hard for her. "Although my future wasn't with a mermaid, it's fitting it's yours. You're a man of the land and the sea."

Falov snorted. "Don't start crying—you're not captain yet. We have to get that heart to the minister first."

Lina scowled, but she grabbed the bag Mora offered her and tucked the Heart inside. "Let's end this fucking thing.

Twenty-One

An ominous, palpable energy flooded over Falov as he entered the minister's home. It was an eerily familiar feeling that made his skin crawl.

Lina was beside him, giving him a skeptical look; her steps punctuated, as if trying to scout the house. She had the satchel with the Heart slung over one shoulder, and a small blade poised in her hand.

They tiptoed on, and Falov's heart was racing so intensely, it was beating in his ears. Where was his mother?

A shattering sound echoed from above, and Falov quickened his pace, racing up the stairs until he was in the last room of the hall. He was greeted with the sight of Syrena on top of a naked man, pointing a blade at his chest, while his mother gripped Syrena's arm, preventing her from making the final push of the knife into flesh. Flashes from last year blinked over his mind, the image before him a replica of the past.

"What the fuck?" Lina hissed from behind him.

Falov saw the strain between his mother and Syrena and how they were battling each other with all their strength. Tears welled in Syrena's eyes.

This time Falov was rational in his decisions. The love of his life was in front of him. He crossed to them, and attempted to ease the blade from Syrena's hand. She turned her head to look at him as he took hold of it, but she wouldn't release the weapon. She had a death grip on it. He could read in her eyes she had one goal in mind, and it was to kill. Her mermaid instincts had kicked in, and she was in a daze of violence.

"Please," he begged quietly. "Please don't." There couldn't be more death.

"They're filthy liars," she growled, the blade inching closer to the minister's trembling body beneath her.

Syrena knew the truth, then. He glanced at his mother, who looked tired, with dark shadows under her eyes. He swallowed. His mother had been through so much over the years. She had lost her first and second husbands. Her son had abandoned her because he selfishly couldn't handle facing the reality of all that had passed.

Falov clasped both his hands around Syrena's hand now. "You'll regret it, Syrena."

"I won't."

Falov pleaded with his eyes for her to let go, for her to see this wasn't the way.

"Nyphadora wouldn't want you to risk yourself like this."

Everyone snapped their attention to Lina, who now had the Heart in her hand. That shock loosened Syrena's grip, and Falov managed to release the blade from her hand, to take it in his own. She climbed off of the minister, and the man immediately sat up, shielding himself with the sheets. Falov kept his eyes on him, making sure he didn't leave. One way or another they needed to give him the Heart—and soon, because time was running out.

"What did you say?" Syrena didn't sound like herself. It was like all her emotions had bubbled out of her mouth, and it led to this deep, despairing voice he didn't recognize.

Lina didn't balk. "Nyphadora learned the truth about the ministers, and she became obsessed with enacting justice for all the seafolk because she had no one who depended on her. Or more accurately, she *thought* she had no one. She went on that mission to kill the minister, uncaring if she was caught or killed. She allowed it to consume her, and she died having changed nothing. Her actions are not something to revere."

"And how would you know so much about Nyphadora?"

"If you learned the truth, it means you found her letters."

Falov's eyes bounced between the two women, watching as Syrena seemed to come to a conclusion, her eyes narrowing at Lina as something clicked into place. "You left her," Syrena seethed. "She loved you, and you left her."

If Falov's eyes were working properly, then he thought he caught a glimpse of a tear rolling down Lina's face, but she wiped it away quickly and gathered herself. "It wouldn't have worked between us.

Nyphadora loved the sea too much, and I loved *The Dark Destiny*. Our love was like a hole in a rowboat. It poured in quickly, and we were overcome with the thought we would be the end for each other. But that boat began to sink when the water reminded us there was more out there for us both. We ended on good terms, and when—" Lina swallowed, her eyes now on Falov, and he tried not to cringe away with shame. "When she died because of unfortunate circumstances that were *nobody's* fault, I thought I would break."

Falov wanted to comfort Lina, but he knew she would hate it so he stayed back. His mother was next to him, her hand on his shoulder.

"I didn't, though, because I was reminded that even in this fucked up world, even when we have been lied to, I realized there isn't much we can do to fight against the Gods or ministers. We're all stuck in this cage—so all we can do is find our own purpose to fulfill us. And I did. I was given a second chance. Don't mess up your chance to live how you want because you decided to allow The Weather Gods and the ministers to rule over your life."

He could tell Syrena wasn't convinced, and he couldn't blame her. It wasn't easy to give up the desire to enact justice.

His mother stepped up, "So you barter instead."

Syrena gave his mother a once-over, almost as if she was confused as to who the person was. Syrena had never met his mother before, but he doubted she wouldn't put it together quickly.

"What do you mean?"

"Ask for what you want."

"Within reason," the minister squeaked. But the fact that he didn't deny what his mother said showed that they perhaps had more control than they'd anticipated. "The Undertakings cannot stop, obviously."

"Then abolish the rule about killing the mermaids for entrance into the Undertaking."

"I said something within reason," he reiterated.

Syrena looked ready to lunge forward, but Falov was there, rubbing the small of her back. *He* was overwhelmed by this encounter, so he couldn't imagine what swirled in Syrena's mind. All he could do was remind her of his presence and how he planned to never leave her side.

"Fine," she gritted through her teeth. Syrena was silent for a moment, her mind an obvious whirlpool as she attempted to settle on an exchange that could possibly make up for what her people were forced to endure. Then her wild eyes turned to the minister, as she said, "The seafolk should be able to keep all the hearts of those that died. Both from the winning and losing teams. We deserve to give our own proper burials."

The minister, who was still sitting in the bed naked under the sheets, stretched out his hand. "I can make that work with the Gods."

Syrena reached out and clasped his hand. They shook on the deal.

"Now...onto why you're here," the minister gestured to the Heart that was still in Lina's hand.

"Oh," Lina went over and handed it to him. "Is that it?"

The minister furrowed his brows.

"I expected something more grand. I almost died like ten times to get that."

The minister did not seem impressed with Lina. "There is a ceremony I do outside on the cliff. An audience I'm sure has formed as we are in the last hours before the end. If you let me get dressed, I will meet you downstairs, and you can attend."

Lina gave him a thumbs up, and they all dispersed from the room, each leaving slightly changed, Falov thought.

Syrena was the last to leave, but Falov had been waiting outside. He cradled her face in his hands. "Are you okay?"

It was such a simple question, yet the answer warred within her mind. She could lie, but she had a feeling he wouldn't accept the answer. Telling the truth sounded exhausting right now because it would only open room for more questions.

She shrugged. "I'm not sure."

It was the most honest thing she could say. Falov pulled her in for a hug, and she reciprocated, taking in his warmth, feeling his heart thudding beneath the layers of clothes and flesh.

They had both survived so much death, and now, perhaps, they could let their grieving hearts rest. Or at least she hoped they could.

They entered the sitting room, where Lina and Falov's mother sat on opposite ends of the room. It was a cozy space, with two wicker couches covered in plush pillows and blankets, a large wooden table at the center where scented candles were lit, emanating a soft vanilla aroma. The fireplace was dark, but she could imagine relaxing in here on a rainy night.

Falov's mother came up to him and enveloped him in a deep hug, leaving Syrena standing awkwardly by his side when he had to let go of her hand.

Lina snorted, and Syrena shot her a sharp look in return.

"I don't see what's so funny. Mermaids will still have to die."

"Someone's always dying. Nyphadora told me the seafolk are always challenging each other to deadly duels for fun. A perk to your quick reproduction rate, I guess."

Syrena's mouth gaped. "It's still not fair that pirates are killing us."

"Then I vow to make it fair," Lina smiled arrogantly, but there was a sadness to those gray eyes. "I can take on a mermaid in a fight."

Syrena crossed her arms. "You're very confident for a landwalker."

"Did Nyphadora not tell you the first time we met was because she tried pick-pocketing me, and I had her on the ground in seconds? When she admitted defeat, she apologized and gave me this necklace," Lina touched the scales around her neck.

"Nyphadora was...different."

Lina hummed her agreement. "She most certainly was."

The room turned solemn, but Falov's hand was in Syrena's again. She rested her head on his shoulder, and she could feel his mother's eyes on her. Although they had never met before, Syrena had heard about her. It wasn't common for a mermaid to give up their tail for love so when one did, it was well known. Syrena admired her, but she didn't know if she would ever be able to do the same. She loved the sea, but she loved Falov, too.

Did he love her in return?

"My son speaks highly of you," his mother said. Those blue eyes—so similar to Falov's—penetrated deeply. Syrena tried not to shift her feet under their scrutiny.

"He's a good one," she managed to respond, and Falov squeezed her hand tighter.

"Promise me you'll take care of each other. The world is not kind to interspecies love."

Falov cleared his throat, but Lina was the one to say. "Even if he's no longer a part of *The Dark Destiny*, he'll always have its protection. That's my pledge as its newly appointed captain."

Syrena whipped her head in his direction. He shrugged. "My future has always had you in it. I never wanted to be captain anyways."

If Syrena saw it clearly, she could have sworn his mother sighed in relief.

"It's time," the minister's voice announced as he joined them, now wearing an emerald green robe. "Do you have the mermaid's heart?"

Falov nodded, and Syrena's instinct was to reach out and take the hourglass herself.

"I promise it will remain intact," the minister said as he took it from Falov.

The minister headed outside the manor, where indeed a small crowd formed. They were overlooking the sea, the gray skies above pouring down on them. Even in the rain, the townspeople wouldn't want to miss a monumental moment like this.

Syrena didn't leave Falov's side, and she wondered if any mermaids were looking up at the edge of the cliff from below. Were they relieved that the Rain Court would survive another year, or resentful of the fact that another year would pass by where mermaids would be killed?

The minister approached a small table, set up like an altar, with gemstones and jewels adorning its surface. He placed two hourglasses side by side: one with Nyphadora's heart, the other empty. Nyphadora's heart was now entirely uncovered from the sand. He removed the lid to the empty side of the second hourglass and placed the emerald Heart within.

The minister said some chants and prayers Syrena didn't listen to, but she watched as he freed Nyphadora's heart from the glass. He cradled the heart in his hands and raised it skyward, thanking Nyphadora for her sacrifice. Then he flipped the second hourglass over, and the sand began to fall, tracking how long until the start of the next Undertaking. Until again mermaids were hunted for a cause they had no say over.

When the minister handed Nyphadora's heart over—the organ no longer beating, and its color drained almost white—Syrena whispered, "I'm taking you home."

Epilogue

Syrena woke up that morning quiet. She moved through the motions without much thought as she prepared herself for the day ahead.

But she wasn't alone. She had spent the night on land in Falov's room of the boarding house where he wrapped his arms around her. It took hours for her eyes to shut, and as every hour passed, she knew Falov was awake with her. She didn't know if he ever fell asleep, but she did know that she was grateful for his comfort.

"Are you sure you want me there?" he asked sincerely, as the golden glow began to seep through the window, casting shadows across his features.

She nodded. "I can't do this without you."

As the town came to life in the morning sun, Falov and Syrena dove into the sea. His bubble formed, and she hoped it lasted long enough for their journey. Falov had reserved his powers for days to elongate the amount of time he could be there with her.

The whole time they swam deeper into the sea, Syrena avoided gazing towards the satchel on his shoulder and what it held.

Her home—a castle of ivory limestone protruding from the seafloor—appeared in the distance. It felt like so long since she had been there, but as soon as she saw it, a wave of calm washed over her.

Falov and Syrena had spent the last few days after the Undertaking talking constantly. He had given up his future role of captain, leaving *The Dark Destiny* so he could focus on his art. He'd received the confidence he needed to move on to the next path in his life. The crew of *The Dark Destiny* were swimming in the praise of the Rain Court and in their treasure, which Syrena did get a cut of, as promised.

When they'd discussed his future, Syrena had worried her lips.

He'd pressed a kiss to her bare shoulder, as they lay together in bed. "I would never let you give up your tail for me."

"Neither the seafolk nor landwalkers will approve. They'll require it."

"They aren't going to arrest us."

"Your mother gave up life at sea for your father, and many other seafolk have done the same. It wouldn't be fair."

"Good thing we can say I found the Heart that allowed us to live another year."

That had been the end of the conversation. She didn't know if his argument would be convincing enough, but the one thing she had learned from all this was that rules could clearly be bent.

They entered the castle, and Syrena was greeted by her mother, who hugged her tightly. Even if she had eight children, her mother had a heart that could hold so much love in it. She pressed a kiss to Falov's cheek.

"Thank you for keeping her safe."

Falov blushed as he watched her mother swim away, and Syrena snorted. "Don't tell me you have a crush on her?"

"What?" he snapped. "Of course not."

Syrena rolled her eyes, but took his hand. They still had a short journey ahead of them, and she didn't want him running out of powers before then.

With each flip of her tail, they neared their destination, and Syrena didn't know if she would ever be ready for it. But Nyphadora deserved this. All the seafolk that had been sacrificed for this court, and that would continue to be, deserved this.

She felt a tug, and she stopped swimming.

Falov wrapped his arms around her waist. "If it's too much, let me know."

She dipped her head to press a kiss, infiltrating his bubble. Their tongues clashed together, desperate for each other's taste.

"I love you," he whispered as he nipped at her bottom lip.

"I know," she gasped, uncaring that they had an audience of other mermaids nearby to see them.

He huffed a laugh on her skin. "Don't hold back on me now."

His hand drifted to her exposed breasts, pinching her peaked nipple. She yelped, but moaned as he massaged the pain away.

She grasped his face with both of her hands, staring deeply into those blue eyes. "You are my heart and soul, Falov. I don't have many left in my life who I let see the deepest parts of me. Of course, I love you."

She wiped the tear that fell on his cheek with her thumb.

"Let's go," he said against her lips.

They held onto each other, and became each other's lifeline, as they reached a special part of the sea that none of the landwalkers knew about—except for one. But his heart was of the sea and land, so he didn't count, she told herself.

The current moved fast, the color of the rainbow glistening brightly as if it knew they would be coming.

"It's beautiful," Falov revered as his eyes widened.

"It leads to the Rafa Reefs," Syrena explained. "Her heart will feed the sea. It's a cycle of life, death, and rebirth. We believe one day all the seafolk will return again as new life. Perhaps in a different shape, but the soul remains the same."

Falov squeezed her hand tightly. "Sometimes I think I see my father. There's a bird that gets too eager about the flaky bread I have—which was his favorite. Sometimes I see him in the art I make."

"They're always with us," Syrena said, her voice shaky.

Falov unclasped the satchel, removing Nyphadora's heart. It had been wrapped in a white sheet, along with Lina's necklace of scales—her own version of goodbye.

"Ready?" Falov asked.

Syrena closed her eyes and breathed. She didn't know how long it took her to get the courage to approach the colorful current, but when she did, she knew she was surrounded by family, the sea, and the one person who would help her get through it all.

"Goodbye, Nyphadora." She let go of the heart, watching as the current took it in its arms and carried it away.

Acknowledgements

Every time I self-publish, the journey gets a little harder. The self-doubt creeps up until its hanging from my shoulder with a death grip I can't shove off. Thankfully, I have people in my corner who make it a worthwhile endeavor.

Thank you to my cover artist Aubrey who always brings her best to the work she does, and I am always so inspired by her dedication to her craft. I am so lucky to have her creating the covers for all these books.

To my editor Des, thank you for absolutely smashing it with your amazing work. They have such a gift for words, and I'm so thankful for the way they enhance my stories.

Lastly, thank you to all the readers—you're the best!

KC Silver is a born and raised Chicagoan who just moved to NYC, where she spends her days exploring the city, one train stop at a time with a sweet treat in hand. She currently works as a media planner at a large media agency where she daydreams of the day when a Slack notification no longer makes her heart jump in fear.

KC enjoys character driven stories where the main character is on a journey of discovering themselves and learning to let go of the expectations weighing on them, while falling in love.

She can be found on all socials @bysilverstories

www.ingramcontent.com/pod-product-compliance
Lightning Source LLC
Chambersburg PA
CBHW032303310726
48973CB00008B/2507